F.

| Date Due | Date Due | Date Due |
|---|---|---|
| 0 4 APR 2018 | | |
| 0 9 JAN 2019 | | |

ANTON CHEKHOV

# THE
# BEAUTIES

*Essential Stories*

Translated from the Russian by
Nicolas Pasternak Slater

PUSHKIN PRESS
LONDON

Pushkin Press
71–75 Shelton Street
London, WC2H 9JQ

English translation © Nicolas Pasternak Slater 2017
This translation first published by Pushkin Press in 2017

1  3  5  7  9  10  8  6  4  2

ISBN 978-1-78227-380-6

Frontispiece: Anton Chekhov on the steps of his house at
Melikhovo, May 1897 © INTERFOTO / Alamy Stock Photo

Typeset by Tetragon, London

Printed and bound in Great Britain by TJ International,
Padstow, Cornwall on Munken Premium White 80gsm

www.pushkinpress.com

# CONTENTS

# THE BEAUTIES

## I

I REMEMBER, when I was a high school boy in the fifth or sixth class, driving with my grandfather from the village of Bolshaya Krepkaya in the Don Region to Rostov-on-Don. It was a wearisomely dreary, sultry August day. The heat and the burning dry wind blew clouds of dust in our faces, gummed up my eyes and dried out my mouth. I didn't feel like looking around, or talking, or thinking; and when Karpo, our drowsy Ukrainian driver, caught my cap with his whip as he lashed his horse, I didn't protest or utter a sound; I just woke from my doze and gazed meekly and dispiritedly into the distance to see if I could make out a village through the dust. We stopped to feed the horse at the house of a rich Armenian whom my grandfather knew, in the big Armenian village of Bakhchi-Salakh. Never in my life had I seen such a caricature of a man as this Armenian. Imagine a small, shaven head with thick beetling eyebrows, a beaky nose, a long grizzled moustache and a wide mouth with a long cherrywood chibouk poking out of it. The little head was clumsily attached to a skinny, hunchbacked body, dressed in fantastic attire – a short red tunic and wide, baggy, bright-blue trousers. This figure walked with his legs wide apart, shuffling along in slippers, talked without taking his chibouk out of his mouth, and carried himself with true Armenian dignity, neither smiling nor staring, but striving to pay his guests as little attention as possible.

There was no wind or dust inside this Armenian's home, but it was just as unpleasant, stifling and dreary as the road and the steppe outside. I remember sitting, covered in dust and worn out by the burning heat, on a green box in a corner. The bare wooden walls, the furniture and the ochre-stained floors all smelt of sun-scorched dry wood. Everywhere you looked there were flies, flies, flies… Grandfather and the Armenian were talking in an undertone about grazing, pastures, sheep… I knew that it would take a whole hour to get the samovar ready, and Grandfather would spend another hour drinking his tea, and then he'd lie down and sleep for two or three hours, and I'd waste a quarter of the day hanging about, after which there would be more heat, and dust, and rattling about in the cart. I listened to the murmur of those two voices and began to feel that the Armenian, and the crockery cupboard, and the flies, and the windows with the hot sun beating in, were all something I had been seeing for a long, long time, and that I would only cease to see them in the far distant future. And I was overcome with loathing for the steppe, and the sun, and the flies…

A Ukrainian peasant woman in a headscarf brought in the tray with the tea things, and then the samovar. The Armenian strolled out onto the porch and called:

"Mashya! Come and pour the tea! Where are you? Mashya!"

There was the sound of hurried footsteps, and in came a girl of about sixteen, in a simple cotton dress and a little white headscarf. As she rinsed the cups and poured out the tea she was standing with her back to me, and all I noticed was that she had a slim waist, her feet were bare, and her little bare heels were covered by the bottoms of her long trousers.

Our host invited me to come and have tea. As I sat down at the table, I glanced at the girl's face while she handed me my glass, and suddenly felt something like a breath of wind over my soul, blowing away all my impressions of the day, with its tedium and dust. I saw the enchanting features of the loveliest face I had ever seen in my waking life, or imagined in my dreams. Before me stood a beauty, and from the very first glance I understood that, as I understand lightning.

I am ready to swear that Masha, or Mashya as her father called her, was a real beauty; but I cannot prove it. It sometimes happens that ragged clouds gather on the horizon, and the sun, hiding behind them, colours them and the sky in every possible hue – crimson, orange, golden, lilac, dusty pink; one cloud looks like a monk, another like a fish, a third like a Turk in a turban. The sunset glow fills a third of the sky, shining on the church cross and the window panes of an elegant house, reflected in the river and the puddles, shimmering on the trees; far, far away against the sunset, a flock of wild ducks flies off to its night's rest… And the farm lad herding his cows, the surveyor driving his chaise over the dam, and the gentlefolk out for their stroll, all gaze at the sunset, and every one of them finds it terribly beautiful, but no one knows or can say what makes it so.

I was not the only one to find this Armenian girl beautiful. My grandfather, an old man of eighty, rough and indifferent to women and the beauties of nature, gazed affectionately at Masha for a whole minute, and asked:

"Is this your daughter, Avet Nazarich?"

"Yes. That's my daughter…" replied our host.

"A fine young lady," said Grandfather appreciatively.

An artist would have called this Armenian girl's beauty classical and severe. It was just the sort of beauty which, as you contemplate it, heaven knows how, fills you with the certainty that the features you are seeing are right – that the hair, eyes, nose, mouth, neck, breast, and all the movements of this young body, have come together in a single, complete harmonic chord, in which nature has committed not the slightest error; you somehow feel that a woman of ideal beauty must possess exactly the same nose as Masha's, straight and slightly aquiline, the same large dark eyes, the same long eyelashes, the same languid look; that her wavy black hair and eyebrows go with the gentle whiteness of her brow and cheeks just as a green rush goes with a quiet stream. Masha's white neck and youthful breast were not yet fully developed, but in order to create them in a sculpture, you feel, one would have to possess an enormous creative talent. You look on, and gradually find yourself wishing to tell Masha something uncommonly agreeable, sincere and beautiful, as beautiful as herself.

At first I was upset and embarrassed that Masha took no notice of me, but kept her eyes lowered; there was, it seemed to me, some special atmosphere of happiness and pride about her that separated her from me, jealously shielding her from my eyes.

"It's because I'm all covered in dust, and sunburnt," I thought, "and because I'm only a boy."

But then I gradually forgot all about myself, and gave myself up wholly to the appreciation of beauty. I no longer remembered the tedium of the steppe, or the dust; I no longer heard the buzzing of the flies, nor noticed the taste of the tea – I was simply aware that opposite me, across the table, there stood a beautiful girl.

I perceived her beauty in a strange sort of way. Masha aroused in me neither desire, nor delight, nor enjoyment, but a strange though pleasant sadness. This sadness was as indeterminate and vague as a dream. For some reason, I felt sorry for myself, and Grandfather, and the Armenian, and the Armenian maiden herself; I felt as if all four of us had lost something important and essential for life, which we would never find again. Grandfather grew sad too. He no longer talked about pastures or sheep, but sat in silence, looking thoughtfully at Masha.

After tea, Grandfather lay down to sleep, while I went out to sit on the porch. This house, like every house in Bakhchi-Salakh, was exposed in full sunlight – there were no trees, or awnings, or shade. The Armenian's great farmyard, overgrown with goosefoot and mallow, was full of life and merriment despite the baking heat. Threshing was in progress behind one of the low wattle fences that ran across the yard here and there. Twelve horses harnessed in line around a post set in the very middle of the threshing floor, and forming a single long radius around it, were trotting round in circles. Beside them walked a Ukrainian in a long tunic and wide trousers, cracking his whip and shouting out as if he meant to taunt the horses and boast of his power over them:

"He-e-ey, you wretches! He-e-ey… go die of cholera! Frightened, are you?"

The chestnut, white and piebald horses had no idea why they were being forced to trot around in circles crushing wheat straw, and they ran unwillingly, forcing themselves on and flicking their tails with a discontented air. The wind raised great clouds of golden chaff from under their hooves, carrying it far away over the fence. Women with rakes jostled one another beside tall, newly built hayricks, carts moved about, and in another yard beyond the hayricks another dozen similar horses trotted around a post, and a second Ukrainian like the first cracked his whip and taunted them.

The steps I was sitting on were hot, and the heat brought sap oozing up out of the flimsy railings and window frames. Little red bugs huddled together in the strips of shade under the steps and behind the shutters. The sun beat down on my head, and my chest, and my back, but I was unaware of it: all I noticed was the padding of bare feet behind me, on the porch and indoors. When Mashya had cleared away the tea things, she ran past me down the steps, fanning the air around me as she passed, and flew like a bird to a little smoke-blackened outhouse, the kitchen I suppose, from which came a smell of roast mutton and the sound of angry Armenian voices. She vanished through the dark doorway, and in her place a hunchbacked old Armenian woman, red-faced and wearing wide green trousers, appeared at the door. She was angrily scolding someone. Soon Mashya reappeared in the doorway, flushed with the heat of the kitchen and carrying a large black loaf on her shoulder. Bending gracefully under its weight, she ran across the yard to the threshing floor, skipped over the fence, and, enveloped by a cloud of golden chaff, disappeared behind the farm carts. The farm hand driving the horses lowered his whip, held his tongue and stood in silence for a minute looking over towards the carts; then, when the Armenian girl once more darted past the horses and skipped over the fence, he followed her with his eyes and shouted at the horses in a most offended voice:

"Hey! Go drop down dead, you devil's brood!"

And all the time after that I went on hearing her bare feet stepping here and there, and saw her crossing and recrossing the farmyard with a serious, troubled expression. Sometimes she ran up or down the steps, fanning me with a breeze as she passed on her way to the kitchen, or the threshing-floor, or out of the gate, and I scarcely had time to turn my head and follow her.

And every time she darted past me in all her beauty, I felt sadder and sadder. I was sorry for myself, and for her, and for the farm hand who followed her with sad eyes every time she ran through the cloud of chaff to the carts. Whether I envied her beauty, or whether I was sorry that this girl was not mine and never would be mine and that I was a stranger to her, or whether I had a vague feeling that her rare beauty was accidental and unnecessary, and like everything on earth, would not last; or whether my sadness was that special feeling aroused when a person contemplates real beauty – God only knows!

Three hours of waiting passed unnoticed. It seemed to me that I hadn't had time to look my fill at Mashya before Karpo had ridden to the river, washed down the horse, and was already harnessing it. The wet horse snorted with pleasure and kicked its hooves against the shafts. Karpo shouted "Ba-a-ack!" Grandfather woke. Mashya opened the creaking gates for us, we took our places in the chaise, and drove out of the yard. We rode in silence, as if angry with one another.

Two or three hours later, when Rostov and Nakhichevan were in sight, Karpo, who had not said a word all the way, looked round quickly and said:

"That's a fine lass, that Armenian's!"

And whipped up his horse.

## II

On another occasion, when I was a student, I was travelling south on the railway. It was May. At one of the stations, I believe between Belgorod and Kharkov, I left my carriage to walk along the platform.

The evening shadows had already descended on the station garden, the platform and the fields around. The sunset was hidden by the station house, but the highest puffs of smoke from the engine, which were now tinted a soft pink, showed that the sun had not yet quite disappeared.

As I strolled up and down the platform, I noticed that most of the passengers out to stretch their legs were strolling or standing in a group beside one particular second-class carriage, with expressions suggesting that some famous person was sitting in it. One of the curious people I encountered near the carriage, incidentally, was a fellow-traveller, an artillery officer – an intelligent, cordial, pleasant fellow, as anyone is whom one chances to meet briefly on a journey.

"What are you looking at there?" I asked.

He did not reply, but just turned his eyes to point out a female figure. This was a young girl of seventeen or eighteen, dressed in Russian costume, bareheaded and wearing a little shawl carelessly slung over one shoulder; not a passenger, but probably the stationmaster's daughter or sister. She was standing next to a carriage window, talking with an elderly lady passenger inside. Before I had time to realize what I was looking at, I was overcome by the same feeling I had once experienced in that Armenian village.

The girl was an amazing beauty, and neither I nor any of the other people looking at her with me was in any doubt about that.

If I was to describe her appearance point by point, as is usually done, then the only truly beautiful thing about her was her thick, wavy fair hair, hanging down and loosely tied with a black ribbon. All the rest was either not quite right, or very commonplace. Whether it was a special way of looking flirtatious, or whether she was short-sighted – her eyes were screwed up, her nose had an uncertain tilt, her mouth was small, her profile weak and indeterminate, her shoulders too narrow for her age; and despite all this, the girl gave the impression of a true beauty, and looking at her, I convinced myself that a Russian face, in order to appear beautiful, does not need to have classically correct features – indeed, if that girl's upturned nose had been replaced by a different one, correct and faultlessly formed like the Armenian girl's, I believe her face would have lost all its charm.

As she stood talking by the window, the girl hunched her shoulders to keep out the cold evening air, kept looking round at us, rested her hands on her hips, lifted them to her head to arrange her hair, talked, laughed, expressed amazement, then shock – I cannot remember a moment when her face and body were at rest. The whole secret, the whole magic of her beauty lay in those slight, supremely elegant movements, her smile, the play of her features, her swift glances at us; in the combination of the fine grace of her movements with her youth, her freshness, the innocence of her soul, that sounded through her laughter and speech; and the vulnerability which we love so much in children, in birds, in young deer or young trees.

It was a moth-like beauty – the beauty that goes so well with a waltz, or darting across a garden, or with laughter and merriment, and which has no business with serious thoughts, sorrow or repose. It seemed as if a good gust of wind blowing along the platform, or a sudden shower, would be enough to make that fragile body suddenly wilt, scattering its capricious beauty like pollen from a flower.

"Ye-es…" sighed the officer, when the second bell sounded and we walked back to our carriage.

What that "Ye-es" meant, I couldn't say.

Perhaps he felt sad, and unwilling to walk away from that beauty, to abandon the spring evening for a stuffy carriage; or perhaps, like me, he felt unaccountably sorry for the beauty, and himself, and me, and all the passengers wandering listlessly and reluctantly back to their compartments. As we passed the station house window, where a telegraphist with upstanding ginger curls and a pale, washed-out face with high cheekbones was sitting at his instrument, the officer said with a sigh:

"I bet the telegraphist is in love with that pretty girl. To live out in the wilds under the same roof as that ethereal creature, and not fall in love – that's beyond the power of man. But what a misfortune, my friend – what a mockery, to be a round-shouldered, shaggy-haired, insignificant, decent fellow, and no fool, and fall in love with that pretty, silly girl, who won't take the slightest notice of you! Or even worse – supposing the telegraphist is in love, but he's already married, and his wife is just as round-shouldered, shaggy and decent as he is… Torture!"

The conductor stood beside our carriage, lolling on the railing between two coaches and looking over to where the beauty was standing. His raddled, flabby, unpleasantly podgy face, worn out by sleepless nights and jolting trains, wore an expression of tenderness and profound sadness, as if in that girl he could see his own youth, happiness, sobriety, purity, his wife and children; as if he was full of regret, and felt with his whole being that this girl was not his, and that he, aged before his time, ungainly and fat-faced, was as far removed from the ordinary, human happiness of us passengers as he was from the sky above.

The third bell rang, whistles sounded, and the train moved slowly off. Past our window there came, first, the conductor, then the stationmaster, then the garden, and the beauty with her wonderful, mischievous, childish smile...

Putting my head out of the window and looking back, I saw her follow the train with her eyes, walk along the platform past the window where the telegraphist sat, pat her hair and run into the garden. The station no longer shut out the western sky, the countryside lay open, but the sun had already set, and black billows of smoke drifted over the velvety green winter corn. There was sadness in the spring air, and the darkening sky, and inside the carriage.

Our own conductor came into the carriage and began lighting the candles.

# THE MAN IN A BOX

I T HAD GROWN LATE, and the hunters settled down for the night in a barn belonging to Prokofy, the village elder, on the very edge of the village of Mironositskoe. There were just two of them: Ivan Ivanich the vet, and Burkin, a high school teacher. Ivan Ivanich had a rather strange double-barrelled surname, Chimsha-Gimalaisky, which didn't suit him in the least, and everyone in the province just knew him as Ivan Ivanich. He lived on a stud farm near the town, and had only come to hunt down here for a breath of fresh air. Burkin the teacher spent every summer as a guest of Count P. and his family, and felt very much at home here.

They were not asleep. Ivan Ivanich, a tall, thin elderly man with a long moustache, sat just outside the door smoking his pipe in the moonlight. Burkin lay inside on the hay, invisible in the dark.

They were telling each other stories. One thing they talked about was how the elder's wife Mavra, a healthy and sensible woman, had never in her life been anywhere outside her native village, never seen a town or a railway, and had spent the last ten years sitting by the stove and only venturing out at night.

"What's so surprising about that?" said Burkin. "There are plenty of people like that, solitary people by nature, who do their best to withdraw into their shell, like a hermit crab or a snail. Maybe that's an atavistic relic, a return to the time when our human ancestors weren't yet social beings, but each lived in his own lair. Or perhaps it's just one variant of human nature – who knows? I'm not a naturalist, and not qualified to talk about that sort of thing; all I mean is that people like Mavra aren't that unusual. In fact you don't have to look far to find an example: there was a teacher of Greek called Belikov, a colleague of mine, who died in my town a couple of months ago. You'll have heard of him, of course. The peculiar thing about him was that whenever he went out, even in the finest weather, he always carried an umbrella and wore galoshes and a warm coat lined with wadding. And he carried his umbrella in a case, and his watch in a grey chamois leather case, and if he took out his penknife to sharpen a pencil, the knife was in a little case too; and it looked as if his face was in a case as well, for he was always hiding it behind a raised collar. He wore dark glasses, and an undervest, and plugged his ears with cotton wool, and if he took a cab, he'd tell the driver to put up the roof. In a word, that man showed a constant, overpowering urge to surround himself with a sort of wrapping, to create an outer box for himself, which would isolate him and protect him from outside influences. Reality upset him, frightened him, kept him in a constant state of alarm; and perhaps it was to justify this timidity on his part, his aversion towards the present time, that he always praised the past, and things which had never been. The ancient languages he taught served essentially the same purpose as his galoshes and umbrella – he used them to hide away from real life.

"'Oh, how resonant, how splendid is the Greek language!' he used to say with a sweet smile. And as if to demonstrate the truth of his words, he would screw up his eyes, point a finger in the air, and pronounce *'Anthropos!'*

"And Belikov tried to hide his thoughts in a case, too. Nothing seemed clear to him except circulars and newspaper articles prohibiting something. If there was a circular forbidding pupils to go out into the streets after nine at night, or if some article proscribed carnal love, that made sense to him. Those things were forbidden, and that was that. Authorizations and permissions, however, always seemed to him to conceal an element of doubt, something vague and not fully expressed. When there were discussions in town about setting up a drama group, or a reading room, or a tearoom, he would shake his head and quietly say:

"'Well, that's all well and good, of course, but it might lead to something…'

"Any kind of infringement, or deviation, or departure from the rules, threw him into gloom, although you might have thought – what business was it of his? If one of his colleagues turned up late for church, or there were rumours about some schoolboy prank, or a schoolmistress was seen walking out with an officer late at night, he'd get very agitated and go on about how it might lead to something. And at the school staff meetings he really got us down, with his caution, his suspicions, his man-in-a-box-like reflections about how the young people in the boys' and girls' high schools were so badly behaved, and very rowdy in class – oh, we mustn't let the authorities hear about it, oh, we must make sure it doesn't lead to anything; and what about expelling Petrov from the second form, and Yegorov from the fourth, that would be an excellent idea. And what happened? With his sighing and moaning, and his dark glasses on that pale little face – you know, a little face like a polecat's – he crushed us all, and we gave in to him, and docked marks off Petrov and Yegorov for bad behaviour, and kept them in, and eventually both Petrov and Yegorov got expelled. And he had a peculiar habit of visiting our lodgings. He'd drop in on a teacher and sit there without saying anything, and he seemed to be watching out for something. He'd sit there for maybe an hour or two, in silence, and then go away. He called that 'keeping up good relations with his colleagues'. And he clearly didn't at all enjoy visiting us and sitting around; the only reason he did it was because he thought it was his duty as a colleague. We teachers were scared of him. Even the headmaster was scared. Just imagine – all our teachers were an intellectual lot, absolutely respectable, brought up on Turgenev and Shchedrin, and yet that man, who always walked about in galoshes and carried an umbrella, kept the whole school under his thumb for fifteen years on end! And not just the school – the whole town! Our wives would never put on amateur dramatics on Saturdays, for fear he'd find out; and the priests didn't dare eat meat or play cards in front of him. It was the influence of Belikov and his sort, over the last ten or fifteen years, that's made everybody in our town afraid of everything now. They're afraid of talking too loud, or sending letters, or making friends, or reading books; they're afraid of helping the poor, or teaching people to read and write…"

Ivan Ivanich coughed and wanted to say something, but first he lit his pipe and looked up at the moon. Then he drawled:

"Yes. Thinking people, respectable people who read Shchedrin, and Turgenev, and Buckle, and all those – and yet they knuckled under and put up with it… That's just the trouble."

"Belikov lived in the same house as me," Burkin went on, "on the same floor, in the flat opposite mine. We often saw one another, and I knew how he lived. And when he was at home, it was the same story: dressing gown, nightcap, shutters on the windows, bolts on the doors, a whole string of prohibitions and restrictions, and oh, supposing it leads to something! Lenten food is bad for you, he thought, but you mustn't eat meat, in case people say that Belikov doesn't keep the fasts, so he'd eat pike-perch cooked in butter, which wasn't Lenten food, but you couldn't call it meat either. He didn't have a maid, in case people thought ill of him, but he had a cook called Afanasy, an old man of sixty or so, half drunk and half crazy, who had once been an officer's batman and more or less knew how to cook. This Afanasy would generally stand by the door, arms folded, endlessly muttering the same thing, with a deep sigh:

"'There's a lot of *them* about these days!'

"Belikov had a small, box-like bedroom, and curtains round the bed. When he got into bed, he'd cover up his head; it was hot and stuffy, and the wind would be rattling the closed doors and howling down the chimney; and there'd be the sound of sighs from the kitchen, ominous sighs...

"And under his blanket, he was scared. Scared of something happening, scared of Afanasy cutting his throat, or burglars getting in; and then he'd have frightening dreams all night, and in the morning, when we walked to school together, he was gloomy and pale, and you could see that the school he was going to, with all those people in it, was frightening and repugnant to his whole being, and that with his solitary nature, he found it unpleasant to walk by my side.

"'They're terribly noisy in class,' he'd say, as if trying to account for his gloom. 'I've never seen anything like it.'

"And would you believe it – that Greek master, that man in a box, almost got married."

Ivan Ivanich quickly looked back into the barn and said:

"You're joking!"

"No, he almost did get married, strange as it seems. They had sent us a new teacher of history and geography, a man called Kovalenko, Mikhail Savvich, a Little Russian. He didn't arrive on his own – he brought his sister Varenka. He was a tall, young, swarthy-faced man with enormous hands, and just to look at his face you could tell that he would talk with a deep voice. And so he did – it sounded like a voice from the bottom of a barrel – boom-boom-boom... And she was past her first youth, about thirty, but tall and graceful as well, with dark eyebrows and pink cheeks; in a word, not a young thing, but a sweetie-pie, and so saucy and noisy, always singing Little Russian songs and giggling. At the slightest thing, she'd burst out in a great laugh – Ha-ha-ha! We first got to know the Kovalenkos properly, I remember, at the headmaster's birthday party. In the midst of all those grim-faced, tense and boring teachers, who wouldn't even have attended a birthday party if they hadn't been obliged to, we suddenly saw this new Aphrodite rising from the foam, walking with her arms akimbo, laughing, singing, dancing... She sang 'The Winds are Blowing', sang it with feeling, and then another song, and another one, and she enchanted us all – everyone, even Belikov. He sat down next to her, simpered in a sugary way and said:

"'The Little Russian language, with its softness and pleasant resonance, is reminiscent of Ancient Greek.'

"She felt flattered, and in a voice full of earnest feeling she started telling him about her farm in Gadyach district, and her mama who lived there, and how it grew such pears, and such watermelons, and such 'kabaks'! The Little Russians call their squashes 'kabak', and what we call 'kabak' – a tavern – they call 'shinka'; and they make a borsch with red and blue squashes, and it's 'so delicious, so delicious, it's simply – terrible!'

"We listened on and on, and suddenly we were all struck by the same thought.

"'What a good idea it would be to get them married,' the headmaster's wife said quietly to me.

"For some reason we all recalled that our Belikov wasn't married, and now we found it strange that we had so far never noticed this important detail of his life, never taken it into account. And what was his attitude to women anyway, how did he approach this vital question for himself? Previously that had never interested us in the least; perhaps we hadn't even admitted the idea that a man who went out wearing galoshes in all weathers, and slept behind bed curtains, could be in love.

"'He's well past forty, and she's thirty…' said the head-master's wife, expanding on her idea. 'I have a feeling she'd take him.'

"What a lot of things get done out of pure boredom, in the provinces – unnecessary, pointless things! And that's because the necessary things aren't done. I mean, why did we have to marry off Belikov all of a sudden, when you couldn't even imagine him married? The headmaster's wife, the inspector's wife, and all our high school ladies perked up, even their looks improved, as if they'd suddenly discovered their aim in life. The headmaster's wife would take a box at the theatre, and we'd look and see Varenka there, holding some kind of fan, glowing with happiness, and by her side there'd be Belikov, a little hunched-up creature, looking as if he'd been extracted from his home with pincers. Or I'd give a party, and straight away the ladies would insist on my inviting Belikov and Varenka. In short, the machine got going. It turned out that Varenka wasn't averse to getting married. She didn't have a very happy life with her brother – all they did was quarrel and shout at one another for days on end. Here's a typical scene: Kovalenko is walking along the street, a tall, healthy young beanpole in an embroidered shirt, his forelock peeping out over his forehead from under his cap, with a pile of books in one hand and a thick knotty stick in the other. His sister is following on behind, also carrying books.

"'But Mikhailik, you've never read this!' she insists loudly. 'I'm telling you, I swear to you, you've never read it at all!'

"'And I'm telling you I have!' shouts Kovalenko, thumping his stick on the pavement.

"'Oh my goodness, Minchik! What are you getting so cross for? This is just a question of principle.'

"'And I tell you I have read it!' Kovalenko shouts even louder.

"And at home, if anybody dropped in, they'd start squabbling. I expect she got fed up with that kind of life, and wanted a place of her own. Besides, you have to remember her age – too late to pick and choose, you'd marry whoever you could, even a Greek master. That's how it is with most of our young ladies – they'll marry anyone, just so long as they get married. Anyway, Varenka obviously began to look kindly on our Belikov.

"And Belikov himself? He used to visit Kovalenko the way he visited us. He'd come in, sit down and say nothing. And while he sat there saying nothing, Varenka would sing him 'The Winds are Blowing', or gaze pensively at him with her dark eyes, or suddenly burst out laughing:

"'Ha-ha-ha!'

"In matters of love, and especially marriage, suggestion plays a big part. Everyone – both his colleagues and the ladies – began assuring Belikov that he had to get married, that there was nothing left for him in life but marriage; we all congratulated him, put on serious faces and mouthed all sorts of platitudes, telling him that marriage was a serious step, and that sort of thing. Besides, Varenka was quite good-looking, interesting, the daughter of a state councillor, with her own farm – and above all, she was the first woman to treat him gently and affectionately. All that put him in a whirl, and he decided that he really did have to get married."

"That would have been the moment to take away his galoshes and umbrella," said Ivan Ivanich.

"Believe it or not, that turned out to be impossible. He stood a portrait of Varenka on his desk, and kept coming round to my place to talk about Varenka, and family life, and how marriage was a serious step; and spent a lot of time visiting the Kovalenkos; but he didn't change his way of life in the least. On the contrary – his decision to get married had a sort of morbid effect on him: he lost weight, became pale, and seemed to retreat even further into his box.

"'I like Varvara Savvishna,' he told me with a faint, twisted little smile, 'and I know that everybody ought to get married, but... all this, you know, has happened rather suddenly... it has to be thought over.'

"'What is there to think about?' I said. 'Just get married, and that's it.'

"'No, marriage is a serious step; one has to weigh up one's obligations and responsibilities... to make sure nothing happens. That worries me such a lot, I no longer sleep at night. And I have to admit that I'm anxious: she and her brother have a strange way of looking at things; they talk, you know, somehow strangely, and she has a very boisterous nature. I might get married, and then, you never know, I could suddenly find myself in some sort of awkward situation.'

"And he didn't propose to her; he kept putting it off, to the great disappointment of the headmaster's wife and all our ladies. He kept weighing up his obligations and responsibilities, and meanwhile he walked out with Varenka almost every day. Perhaps he thought that was what one had to do in his position. And he'd come round to see me and talk about family life. And in all probability, he'd have ended up proposing to her, and that would have led to one of those stupid, unnecessary marriages that happen by the thousand among us, out of boredom and idleness, if there hadn't suddenly been a *kolossalische Skandal*. I have to explain that Varenka's brother, Kovalenko, had taken an instant dislike to Belikov on the very first day they met, and loathed him.

"'I can't understand,' he'd say to us, shrugging his shoulders, 'I can't understand how you can stomach that sneak, with his ugly mug. Oh, my friends, how can you manage to go on living here? The atmosphere all around you is stifling, it's poisonous. Call yourselves schoolmasters, teachers? You're office clerks! It's not a temple of knowledge you have here, it's a department of correct behaviour, and it stinks as sour as a police box. No, my friends, I'll stay with you a little bit longer, and then I'll be off to my farm, to catch crayfish and teach the Little Russian children. I'll go, and you can stay here with that Judas of yours, God rot him!'

"Or else he'd laugh and chortle till the tears came to his eyes, now in his deep bass voice, now in a thin, shrill squeak, throwing out his arms wide and asking me:

"'Why's he always sitting around at my place? What does he want? Sitting and gawping...'

"He even gave Belikov a nickname, The Bloodsucker or The Spider. Obviously we avoided talking to him about how his sister Varenka was going to marry this Bloodsucker or Spider. And when the headmaster's wife suggested to him one day that it would be a good idea to marry his sister off to such a sound, universally respected man as Belikov, he scowled and grumbled:

"'Not my business. She can marry a viper if she wants; I don't like meddling in other people's affairs.'

"Now listen to what happened next. Some joker drew a caricature of Belikov, walking along in his galoshes, with his trousers rolled up and his umbrella over his head, arm in arm with Varenka; and the caption under the picture was 'Anthropos in Love'. The artist had captured his expression, you know, extraordinarily well. He must have worked on it several evenings on end, because all the teachers at the boys' and girls' high schools, and the ones at the seminary, and the officials – every one of them got a copy. Belikov got one too. That caricature upset him dreadfully.

"We left the house together – it was May Day, a Sunday, and all of us, teachers and pupils, had arranged to meet at the school and then go for a walk together out of town, to the woods. So we went out, and he was looking green, darker than a thundercloud.

"'What wicked, evil people there are!' he said through trembling lips.

"I even felt sorry for him. So we were walking along, and suddenly, just imagine, Kovalenko comes bowling along on a bicycle, with Varenka following behind on a bicycle too, red in the face and tired out, but merry and cheerful all the same.

"'We'll beat you there!' she cries. 'The weather's so lovely, so lovely – it's terrible!'

"And they both disappeared from sight. My Belikov turned from green to white and seemed to go rigid. He stopped dead and stared at me.

"'Excuse me, but what's the meaning of that?' he demanded. 'Or were my eyes perhaps deceiving me? Is it proper for high school teachers and women to ride on bicycles?'

"'What's improper about it?' I said. 'Let them ride around, and good luck to them.'

"'What on earth do you mean?' he shouted, amazed to see me so calm. 'Whatever are you saying?'

"He was so shocked that he refused to go any further, and turned back home.

"Next day he kept nervously rubbing his hands and twitching, and you could see by his face that he wasn't well. He stayed away from work, which was the first time in his life that had happened to him. And ate nothing. That evening he dressed very warmly, though it was high summer outside, and trudged over to the Kovalenkos. Varenka was out, and he only found her brother at home.

"'Do sit down, please,' said Kovalenko coldly, with a frown. His face was sleepy; he had just been having his after-dinner nap, and was very much out of temper.

"Belikov sat in silence for ten minutes or so, and then began:

"'I have come to see you to relieve my mind. I am very, very distressed. Some scribbler has made a drawing that ridicules me and another individual who is close to both of us. I regard it as my duty to assure you that I had no part in this... I have given no grounds for such mockery – on the contrary, I have always conducted myself as a perfect gentleman.'

"Kovalenko sat there scowling and said nothing. Belikov waited a little, and then went on in a quiet, mournful voice:

"'And I have something further to say to you. I have been in service for a long time, while you have only recently entered it, and I regard it as my duty, as an older colleague, to put you on your guard. You ride on a bicycle, a pastime that is entirely unsuitable for an educator of youth.'

"'Why is that?' asked Kovalenko in his bass voice.

"'What need is there of explanations, Mikhail Savvich? Is it not obvious? If a teacher rides on a bicycle, what is there left for the pupils to do? All that remains is for them to walk on their heads! Since this is not authorized by official circular, it is forbidden. I was horrified yesterday! When I saw your sister, everything went black before my eyes. A woman, or a girl, on a bicycle – that is horrible!'

"'What is it exactly that you want?'

"'All that I want is one thing – to warn you, Mikhail Savvich. You are a young man, you have your future before you, and you need to conduct yourself very, very carefully – but you are going wrong, oh, so very wrong! You go about in an embroidered shirt, you're always carrying some sort of books with you in the street, and now here's this bicycle too. The fact that you and your sister ride on bicycles will come to the notice of the headmaster, and then the supervisor... What is the good of that?'

"'The fact that my sister and I ride bicycles is nobody's business!' said Kovalenko, turning crimson in the face. 'And if anybody meddles in my home and family affairs, I'll pack him straight off to the devil.'

"Belikov turned pale and got up.

"'If you talk to me in that tone, I cannot continue,' he said. 'And I request you never to use such language about our superiors in my presence. The authorities must be treated with respect.'

"'Was I saying anything bad about the authorities?' demanded Kovalenko, glaring furiously at him. 'Kindly leave me alone. I'm an honest man and don't want anything to do with a gentleman of your sort. I don't like sneaks.'

"Belikov fell into a nervous flutter and started hurriedly putting on his coat, a horrified expression on his face. This was the first time in his life he had been subjected to such rudeness.

"'You may say whatever you please,' he said, stepping out from the hallway onto the landing. 'But I must warn you that we may have been overheard, and in order to ensure that our conversation is not misrepresented, which might perhaps lead to something, I shall be obliged to report the content of our conversation to the headmaster... in its essential terms. It is my duty to do so.'

"'Report it? Go on, then, report it!'

"Kovalenko seized him by the collar from behind, and gave him a shove. Belikov tumbled down the stairs, his galoshes clattering against the steps. The staircase was tall and steep, but he reached the bottom without injury. He picked himself up and felt his nose, to make sure his spectacles were undamaged. But at the very moment when he was tumbling downstairs, Varenka came in with two other ladies. They stood at the bottom of the stairs and watched – and for Belikov that was the most terrible thing of all. It might have been better for him to break his neck and both legs, rather than become a laughing stock. For now the whole town would find out, and it would reach the headmaster, and the supervisor – and oh, what might that lead to! – and someone would draw another caricature, and it would all end with him being ordered to resign his post…

"When he got up, Varenka recognized him, and seeing his comical face, and crumpled coat, and galoshes, and not realizing what had happened, she supposed that he had accidentally fallen downstairs, and unable to restrain herself, she burst out laughing so loudly that the whole house could hear her:

"'Ha-ha-ha!'

"And that pealing, rolling 'Ha-ha-ha' put an end to everything – to Belikov's courtship, and his earthly existence. He didn't hear what Varenka was saying, nor see anything. Returning home, he first of all removed the portrait from his desk, and then went to bed, never to get up again.

"Three days later Afanasy came to see me and asked whether he ought to send for the doctor, because there was something wrong with his master. I went to see Belikov. He was lying in bed with the curtains drawn, covered with a blanket, and not speaking. If you asked him a question, he'd just say yes or no, and not another sound. He lay there, with Afanasy prowling around, gloomy, scowling, sighing deeply – and stinking of vodka like a pothouse.

"A month later Belikov died. We all went to his funeral – both the high schools, and the seminary. Now, as he lay in his coffin, he had a pleasant, meek, even happy expression on his face, as if he was glad that he had finally been laid in a box from which he would never emerge. Yes, he had achieved his ideal! And as though in honour of him, the weather at his funeral was dull and wet, and we were all in our galoshes and carrying umbrellas. Varenka also attended the funeral, and when the coffin was being lowered into the grave, she burst into tears. I have observed that Little Russian women are always either weeping or laughing; they don't have a mood in between.

"I must confess that burying people like Belikov is a great pleasure. Coming back from the cemetery we all wore meek Lenten faces – nobody wanted to betray that sense of pleasure, a feeling like the one we used to have, long, long ago, in our childhood, when the grown-ups went out and we could run around the garden for an hour or two, revelling in our complete freedom. Ah, freedom, freedom! Even a hint of it, even the faint hope of its possibility, gives your soul wings, doesn't it?

"We arrived back from the cemetery in good spirits. But no more than a week had passed before our lives once more became just as they had been before – gloomy, exhausting and pointless; lives not forbidden by official circular, but not entirely permitted either. Things were no better. And indeed, Belikov was buried, but what a lot of these men in boxes there still are, and how many more are yet to come!"

"Well, that's just it," said Ivan Ivanich, lighting his pipe.

"How many more yet to come!" repeated Burkin.

The schoolteacher stepped out of the barn. He was a man of medium height, plump, completely bald, with a black beard descending almost to his waist. The two dogs came out with him.

"What a moon, what a moon!" he said, looking upwards.

It was already midnight. To his right, the whole village could be seen, with its long street stretching some four miles into the distance. Everything was buried in deep, quiet sleep – not a movement, not a sound. It was hard to believe that such a silence could exist in nature. When you see a broad village street by moonlight, with its huts, haystacks and slumbering willow trees, peace descends on your soul. When it is surrounded by such tranquillity, sheltered from its labours, cares and sorrows by the shadows of night, it feels meek, melancholy and beautiful, as if even the stars are gazing down on it with tenderness and love, and there is no more wickedness on earth, and all is well. To the left, beyond the end of the village, the fields began; they could be seen stretching far away to the horizon, and here too, in all this expanse of moonlit countryside, there was not a movement, not a sound.

"That's just it," repeated Ivan Ivanich. "But aren't we ourselves, living in stuffy towns, in cramped conditions, writing pointless papers, playing at vint – aren't we living in boxes too? And the way we spend our whole lives surrounded by idle, petty men and vain, stupid women, talking and listening to all sorts of rubbish – isn't that living in a box? I can tell you a very instructive story, if you like."

"No, it's time to go to sleep," said Burkin. "Let's talk tomorrow!"

They both went into the barn and lay down on the hay. And they had both covered themselves up and fallen into a doze when they heard light footsteps: tap, tap… Someone was walking about near the barn, going a few steps and stopping, then starting off again a minute later: tap, tap… The dogs growled.

"That's Mavra," said Burkin.

The footsteps died away.

"You see them and hear them telling all those lies," said Ivan Ivanich, rolling over, "and they call you a fool for putting up with their lies; and you swallow insults and humiliations, and don't dare speak out and say that you're on the side of honest, free people; and you tell lies yourself, and smile, and all for the sake of a piece of bread and a warm corner to sit in, all for some stupid promotion that isn't worth having – no, we can't go on living like this!"

"Well, now you're off on a different tack, Ivan Ivanich," said the schoolmaster. "Let's go to sleep."

Ten minutes later Burkin was asleep. But Ivan Ivanich kept turning over from one side to the other and sighing, and eventually he got up, stepped outside again, sat down by the door and lit his pipe.

## A DAY IN THE COUNTRY

I T IS PAST eight o'clock in the morning.
A dark leaden mass is creeping towards the sun. Here and there, jagged streaks of red lightning flicker across it. Thunder rumbles in the distance. A warm wind plays over the grass, bending the trees and lifting the dust. In another minute the May rain will splash down and the real thunderstorm will begin.

Fiokla the six-year-old beggar girl is running barefoot through the village, looking for Terenty the cobbler. The white-haired little girl is pale, with wide eyes and trembling lips.

"Uncle dear, where's Terenty?" she asks everyone she meets. Nobody tells her. They are all nervous of the coming storm, and hurrying to their huts for shelter. Eventually she meets Silanty Silych the sacristan, a good friend of Terenty's. He's walking along, staggering in the wind.

"Uncle dear, where's Terenty?"

"In the kitchen gardens," Silanty replies.

The little beggar girl runs out past the huts to the kitchen gardens and finds Terenty there. Terenty the cobbler, a tall old man with a thin pockmarked face and very long legs, barefoot and wearing a torn woman's jacket, is standing by the vegetable beds gazing with bleary, tipsy eyes at the dark storm cloud. He looks like a crane on his long legs, and in the wind he's shaking like a birdhouse on a pole.

"Uncle Terenty!" says the white-haired beggar girl. "Uncle, darling!"

Terenty bends down to Fiokla, and a smile spreads over his solemn, drunken face, the way people smile when they come across something small, silly, funny, but deeply loved.

"Aha! Fiokla, God's servant!" he says, lisping tenderly. "Where have you sprung from?"

"Uncle Terenty, dear," sobs Fiokla, hanging on to the cobbler's coat-tails. "My brother Danilka's had a terrible accident! Come on!"

"What sort of accident? O-ooh, what a thunderclap! Holy, holy, holy… What accident?"

"Danilka was in the count's wood and he pushed his hand down a hole in a tree, and now he can't get it out. Come on, uncle dear, get it out for him, do, please!"

"How did he get his hand stuck there? What for?"

"He wanted to get a cuckoo's egg out of the hole for me."

"The day's hardly started, and you two are already in trouble…" says Terenty. He shakes his head and spits thoughtfully. "Well, what am I to do with you now? We've got to go… Got to… The wolf ought to gobble you up, you mischief-makers! Come along, little orphan!"

Terenty leaves the kitchen garden, and raising his long legs high above the ground, strides out along the road. He walks quickly, without looking to either side and without stopping, as though he's being pushed from behind or is scared of being pursued. Fiokla the little beggar girl can hardly keep up with him.

The travellers leave the village behind them and follow the dusty road to the count's wood, which shows blue in the distance. It must be a mile and a half away. Meanwhile the storm clouds have hidden the sun, and soon there won't be a scrap of blue left in the sky. It's getting darker.

"Holy, holy, holy," whispers Fiokla, hurrying after Terenty.

The first big heavy raindrops splash down, making dark spots on the dusty road. A large drop falls onto Fiokla's cheek and trickles down to her chin like a teardrop.

"It's started raining!" mutters the cobbler, kicking up the dust with his bare bony feet. "Thank God for that, Fiokla, old thing. The grass and trees feed on rain the way you and I feed on bread. And as for that thunder, don't you worry, little orphan. Why would it want to kill a little thing like you?"

Now that the rain has started, the wind drops. There's only the sound of the rain, pattering down like fine shot onto the young rye and the dry road.

"We're going to be soaked through, you and I, Feklushka!" mutters Terenty. "There won't be a dry patch

45

on us anywhere! Oho, my friend! It's trickling down my neck! But don't you worry, you silly... The grass'll dry out, the earth'll dry out, and we'll dry out too. The sun's there just the same for everyone."

A bolt of lightning fifteen feet long flashes above the travellers' heads. There's a rumbling peal of thunder, and Fiokla has the feeling that something big, round and heavy is rolling around in the sky, tearing holes in it right over her head!

"Holy, holy, holy..." says Terenty, crossing himself. "Don't be afraid, little orphan! It's not thundering out of spite."

The cobbler's feet and Fiokla's feet are getting covered in lumps of heavy wet clay. Walking is difficult and slippery, but Terenty strides out faster and faster... The weak little beggar girl is panting, ready to drop.

But now at last they've reached the count's wood. The trees, washed clean and now shaken by a sudden gust of wind, spray them with a shower of raindrops. Terenty stumbles over tree stumps and slows his pace.

"Where's Danilka?" he asks. "Take me to him!"

Fiokla leads him further into the thicket, and after a quarter of a mile she points to her brother Danilka. Her brother is a small boy of eight with ochre-coloured sandy hair and a pale, sickly face. He's standing pressed against a tree, his head tilted sideways, squinting up at the sky. One of his hands is clutching a worn little cap; the other is hidden down a hole in the old lime tree. The boy is staring hard at the stormy sky, and doesn't seem to be aware of his predicament. When he hears footsteps and sees the cobbler, he gives a wan smile and says:

"What a terrible thunderstorm, Terenty! I've never heard thunder like this in my life…"

"Where's your hand?"

"Down this hole… Do get it out, please, Terenty!"

The edge of the hole has cracked and caught Danilka's hand: he can push it further in, but he can't manage to pull it back. Terenty breaks off the cracked piece, and the boy's hand, squashed and red, comes free.

"What terrible thunder!" repeats the boy, rubbing his hand. "Why does it thunder, Terenty?"

"It's one storm cloud running up against another…" says the cobbler.

The three of them leave the trees behind and walk by the edge of the wood to the black stripe of the road. Gradually the storm dies away, and the rolls of thunder sound far off, beyond the village.

"Terenty, some ducks flew by here the other day…" says Danilka, still rubbing his hand. "They must have settled in the marshes at Foul Meadows. Fiokla, would you like me to show you a nightingale's nest?"

"Don't touch it, you'll disturb them…" says Terenty, wringing water out of his cap. "The nightingale's a song-bird, he has no sin… he's been given that voice in his throat to praise God and gladden mankind. It's sinful to disturb him."

"What about a sparrow?"

"A sparrow doesn't matter. He's a wicked, spiteful bird. All he thinks about is stealing. He doesn't like people to be happy. When they were crucifying Christ, he brought nails to the Jews and sang out 'Alive! Alive!'…"

A light blue speck appears in the sky.

"Look at that!" says Terenty. "The rain's burst open an anthill! It's drowned those rascals!"

They bend over the anthill. The downpour has washed away the ants' dwelling, and the insects are running about in dismay, ministering to their drowned fellows.

"Don't you fret, it won't kill you," says the cobbler with a grin. "As soon as the sun warms you up, you'll come back to life again… Let that be a lesson to you, you fools. Don't set up house on low ground next time…"

They walk on.

"Here are some bees!" cries Danilka, pointing at a branch of a young oak.

The bees, soaked and chilled through, are huddled tightly together on the branch. There are so many that neither bark nor leaves can be seen. Many of them have settled on top of one another.

"That's a swarm," explains Terenty. "They were all flying around, looking for a home, and when the rain fell on them, they settled. If a swarm's in the air, all you have to do is splash some water on them and they'll settle. And then, supposing you want to take them, you lower the branch they're on into a sack and give it a shake, and they all fall in."

Little Fiokla suddenly grimaces and scratches roughly at her neck. Her brother looks at her neck and sees a big blister there.

"Heh-heh!" laughs the cobbler. "Fiokla, my friend, do you know where you got that lump from? Somewhere in that thicket there are some Spanish flies on one of the trees. And the water trickled off them and dripped onto your neck – and that's what gave you your blister."

The sun comes out from behind the clouds, and the woods, the fields and our three wanderers bask in its light and warmth. The dark storm cloud has gone far away, taking the thunder with it. The air grows warm and fragrant. It smells of bird cherries, meadowsweet and lilies of the valley.

"They give you that herb if you have a nosebleed," says Terenty, pointing to a furry flower. "It helps."

There's a whistle and a rumble, but it's not the same rumble as the one that the clouds have just carried away. A goods train races past in front of Terenty's, Danilka's and Fiokla's eyes. The engine, puffing and belching out black smoke, is pulling more than twenty trucks behind it. It's amazingly powerful. The children would like to know how a railway engine, which isn't alive and has no horses to help it, can move along and drag such a weight with it; and Terenty sets out to explain it to them:

"It's all to do with the steam, children... The steam works... So it presses under that thing next to the wheels, and that's... what I mean... that's what makes it go..."

The three of them cross the railway track and walk down the embankment towards the river. They're not going for any particular reason, just following their noses, talking all the way. Danilka asks questions, and Terenty answers them...

Terenty answers all the questions; there isn't a mystery in the whole of nature that can stump him. He knows everything. He knows the names of all the grasses in the fields, and all the animals and stones. He knows which herbs are used to cure diseases, and has no difficulty telling the age of a horse or a cow. By looking at the sunset, or the moon, or the birds, he can tell what the weather will be like tomorrow. And it isn't just Terenty who's so knowledgeable. Silanty Silych, and the innkeeper, the market gardener, the shepherd, in fact the whole village – everyone knows just as much as he does. Those people haven't learnt from books, but from the fields, the woods, and the riverbanks. The birds themselves taught them as they sang their songs, and the sun as it set and left a crimson glow behind it, and the very trees and grasses too.

Danilka watches Terenty and eagerly takes in every word. In the springtime, when the warmth and the monotonous green of the fields haven't yet grown stale for us, when everything is new and breathes freshness, who wouldn't be interested to hear about golden May beetles, or cranes, or wheat coming into ear, or gurgling brooks?

The two of them, cobbler and orphan, walk through the fields, talking endlessly, never tiring. They could happily wander the wide world for ever. As they walk, deep in conversation about the beauty of the earth, they don't notice the frail little beggar-girl hurrying along after them. She's trudging along, driving herself on, and getting breathless. There are tears in her eyes. She'd be happy to abandon these tireless wanderers, but where could she go, and to whom? She has neither home nor family. So, willy-nilly, she has to follow along and listen to the conversation.

A little before midday, all three sit down on the river-bank. Danilka reaches into his bag to take out a piece of bread, sodden and reduced to porridge, and the wanderers begin to eat. When he's had his bread, Terenty says a prayer, then stretches out on the sandy bank and falls asleep. While he's asleep, the boy watches the water and thinks. All sorts of thoughts come into his head. Today he's seen a thunderstorm, bees, ants, and a train, and now there are little fishes darting busily about before his eyes. Some are a couple of inches long or more, others no bigger than a fingernail. And an adder, with its head held high, is swimming from one bank to the other.

Not until evening do our wanderers return to the village. The children go to spend the night in an abandoned barn which was once used to store the communal grain; Terenty bids them good night and goes off to the tavern. The children huddle together on the straw and fall into a doze.

The boy isn't asleep. He's gazing into the darkness, and it seems to him that he can see everything that he saw today: the storm clouds, the bright sun, the birds, the little fishes, and lanky Terenty. All this mass of different impressions, and his exhaustion and hunger, take their toll. He's burning as though on fire, and rolling over from side to side. He wants to tell someone everything he's now imagining in the darkness, everything that's making his thoughts race; but there's no one to tell. Fiokla is still too small, she'd never understand.

"I'll be sure and tell Terenty tomorrow..." thinks the boy.

The children fall asleep, thinking about the homeless cobbler. And in the night-time Terenty comes to them, makes the sign of the cross over them, and lays some bread by their heads. Nobody sees that love. Nobody, save perhaps the moon, as it sails across the sky and peeps tenderly through the holes in the eaves into the derelict barn.

# A BLUNDER

Ilya sergeyich peplov and his wife Kleopatra
Petrovna stood behind the door, listening eagerly.
Inside, in the little parlour, a declaration of love seemed
to be in progress between their daughter, Natashenka, and
Schupkin, a teacher at the local school.

"He's taking the bait!" whispered Peplov, trembling
with impatience and rubbing his hands. "Now you watch
it, Petrovna, the moment they start talking about their
feelings, you get the icon down from the wall and we'll go
in and bless them… catch them at it… A blessing with an
icon is sacred and inviolable… He won't get away after
that, not even if he goes to law."

Inside the room, the following conversation was
going on:

"Stop being like that," said Schupkin, striking a match
against his checked breeches. "I never wrote you any
letters!"

"Oh, yes! As if I didn't know your handwriting!" giggled
the young lady, with an affected squeal, as she examined
herself in the mirror. "I knew you right away! And what a

peculiar man you are! You teach calligraphy, but you write like a farmyard chicken! How can you teach handwriting when your own is so awful?"

"Hm! That doesn't mean a thing. The main point about teaching calligraphy isn't the actual handwriting, it's making sure the pupils don't misbehave. Some of them you have to smack on the head with a ruler, others you smack on the knees… Anyway, what's handwriting? A waste of time! Nekrasov was a writer, but the way he wrote was a disgrace. They show his handwriting in his *Collected Works*."

"Nekrasov's one thing, you're another." (Sigh.) "I'd be happy to marry a writer. He'd always be writing me poems."

"I'll write you a poem if you like."

"What can you write about?"

"Love… feelings… your eyes… When you read it, you'll be overwhelmed… You'll have tears in your eyes! So, if I write you some poetic verses, will you let me kiss your hand?"

"What a fuss over nothing!… Kiss it here and now, if you like!"

Schupkin sprang up, wide-eyed, and knelt down to that plump hand that smelt of egg soap.

"Get the icon down," said Peplov hurriedly, nudging his wife with his elbow. Pale with excitement, he buttoned up his coat. "Let's go! Come on!"

And without a second's delay, Peplov flung open the door.

"My children…" he quavered, raising his hands and blinking tearful eyes. "The Lord bless you, my children… Live happy… be fruitful and multiply…"

"And I bless you too…" said Mama, weeping with joy. "Be happy, my dears! Ah, you're robbing me of my only treasure!" she went on, turning to Schupkin. "Love my daughter, care for her…"

Schupkin gaped in astonishment and terror. This onslaught by the two parents had been so sudden and daring, he couldn't bring out a single word.

"They've got me surrounded!" he thought, feeling faint with horror. "You're done for, brother! No escape!"

And he humbly lowered his head for the blessing, as if to say: "Take me, I'm beaten!"

"I bless… bless you…" began Papa, and he also burst into tears. "Natashenka, my daughter… come and stand beside him… Petrovna, pass me the icon…"

But then Papa suddenly stopped crying, and his face twisted with fury.

"Blockhead!" he snapped angrily at his wife. "You stupid ass! What sort of icon is this?"

"O blessed Saints above!"

What had happened? Timidly the calligraphy teacher raised his eyes and saw that he was saved. Instead of the icon, Mama in her haste had snatched down from the wall a portrait of the writer Lazhechnikov. Old Peplov and his spouse Kleopatra Petrovna stood there all abashed, holding the portrait in their hands, not knowing what to say or do. The calligraphy teacher made the most of the confusion and took to his heels.

# ABOUT LOVE

A T LUNCH NEXT DAY they were served delicious little
pies, crayfish and mutton cutlets; and while they were
eating, Nikanor the cook came up to ask what the guests
would like for dinner. He was a man of medium height
with a puffy face and small eyes, and so clean-shaven that
his whiskers seemed to have been plucked out by the roots
rather than shaved off.

Aliokhin said that the beautiful Pelageya was in love
with this cook. As he was a drunkard and a brawler, she
had refused to marry him, but was willing just to live with
him. But he was very devout, and his religious beliefs didn't
allow him to live with her like that; he insisted that she must
marry him, didn't want her on any other terms, and when
he was drunk he would swear at her and even beat her.
When he was drunk she would hide upstairs, sobbing, and
then Aliokhin and the servants wouldn't leave the house,
in case she needed their protection.

The conversation turned to love.

"How love is born," said Aliokhin, "and why Pelageya
didn't fall in love with someone else, more of a match for

her mind and her looks – why she had to fall in love with Nikanor, that snout-face – everyone round here calls him snout-face – when love involves vital questions about a person's happiness – those are things that no one understands, and you can say what you like about them. There's only one indisputable truth that's ever been told about love, and that's 'this is a great mystery'. Anything else that's been written or said about love hasn't answered any questions, but just restated them, and they still haven't ever been resolved. Any explanation that seems to do for one case will be useless for a dozen others, and I think the best thing is to explain each case on its own merits, without trying to generalize. As the doctors put it, we have to individualize each separate case."

"Quite right," agreed Burkin.

"We Russians, educated people I mean, simply love such questions with no answers. Love generally gets poeticized, adorned with roses and nightingales; but we Russians adorn our love with these fateful questions – and what's more, we choose the least interesting ones. In Moscow, while I was still a student, I had a lover, a charming lady, and whenever I held her in my arms she'd always be wondering how much I'd be giving her a month, and what beef cost per pound just then. And we too, when we're in love, never stop asking ourselves questions – whether this is honourable or dishonourable, sensible or stupid, where this love is leading, and so forth. Whether all that's good or not I don't know, but I do know that it's unsatisfying and upsetting and gets in our way."

It looked as if he was about to tell us a story. People who live alone always have something on their mind that they'd like to talk about. In town, bachelors go to the bathhouse or the restaurant just to chat, and sometimes they tell the bathhouse attendants or the waiters very interesting stories; in the country they generally pour out their souls to their guests. Outside the windows there was a grey sky and rain-sodden trees; in weather like that, there was nowhere to go and nothing to do but tell stories and listen to them.

"I live at Sofyino and I've been farming for years," began Aliokhin; "ever since I left university. I was brought up to do nothing, and I would have liked to devote myself to study, but the estate, when I came here, was deep in debt; and since my father had run into debt partly through spending a great deal on my education, I decided that I wouldn't leave, but would work until I'd paid off the debt. Having taken that decision, I started working here, and I must confess that it rather repelled me. The soil here doesn't yield much, and in order to turn a profit from your farming you have to use either serfs or hired labourers, which amounts to practically the same thing; or else run your estate the way the peasants do – I mean, work in the fields yourself, with your family. There's no middle way. But at the time I didn't get into such subtle arguments. I didn't leave a single clod of earth unturned,

I brought in all the peasants, men and women, from the villages around, and the work carried on at a frantic pace. I went out ploughing myself, and sowing, and reaping, and it bored me, and I had the same disgusted expression on my face as a village cat that's so hungry it's reduced to eating cucumbers from the kitchen garden. My whole body ached; I slept as I walked. At first I thought I could easily reconcile such a life of labour with my habits as a cultured man; all I had to do, I thought, was maintain a semblance of order in my life. I made my home upstairs here, in the best rooms, and arranged to have coffee and liqueurs brought to me after lunch and dinner, and when I went to bed I read the *European Messenger* every night. But one day Father Ivan, our priest, dropped in, and drank up all my liqueurs at a single sitting; and the *European Messenger* went to the priest's daughters too, since in summertime, particularly during haymaking, I never had time to go to bed, but lay down to sleep on a sledge in the barn, or in a forest hut – how could I have done any reading? Bit by bit I've moved downstairs, and started eating in the servants' kitchen, and all I have left of my former luxury is these servants, who've been here since my father's time and whom I can't bear to send away.

"Near the beginning of my time here I was elected an honorary justice of the peace. Occasionally I had to go to town for meetings of the committee and the district court, and that was a change of scene for me. When you spend two or three months living here without a break, particularly in winter, you eventually find yourself longing for a black frock coat. And the district court had frock coats, and uniforms, and tailcoats – nothing but lawyers, people with a broad education. There was somebody to talk to. After sleeping in a sledge and eating in the servants' kitchen, the chance to sit in an armchair wearing clean linen and light boots, with a chain on one's chest, was such a luxury!

"People in town gave me a warm welcome, and I was eager to make new friends. And of all my friendships there, the closest and, I must say, the pleasantest for me was my friendship with Luganovich, the deputy chairman of the district court. You both know him: he's an absolutely charming person. That happened just after the famous case of the arsonists: the investigation had gone on for two days, and we were exhausted. Luganovich looked at me and said:

"'Do you know what? Let's go and dine at my home.'

"That was unexpected, since I didn't know Luganovich well, I had only met him officially, and I'd never been to his home. I looked in at my lodgings for a minute to change, and set off to dinner. And that was where it came about that I met Luganovich's wife, Anna Alexeyevna. She was still very young then, no more than twenty-two, and she'd had her first child six months before. All that's in the past, and right now I'd have trouble deciding what exactly it was that was so unusual in her – what appealed to me so much. But at the time, at dinner, everything was absolutely clear to me. I was looking at a woman who was young, beautiful, kind, cultured, and fascinating, a woman like no one I had ever met before; and I instantly felt that this was someone close to me, someone already familiar – as if I had once seen that face, with its friendly, intelligent eyes, at some time in my childhood, in the album that lay on my mother's chest of drawers.

"Four Jews had been charged in the arson case, accused of being a criminal gang, and as far as I could see there was no case against them. At dinner I became very agitated and upset; I can't remember what I said, only Anna Alexeyevna kept shaking her head and asking her husband:

"'Dmitry, how can that happen?'

"Luganovich was a good fellow, one of those simple souls who cling firmly to the view that if someone lands up in court, that means he's guilty, and that one can't express any doubts about the fairness of the sentence except in legal form, on paper – certainly not in a private conversation over dinner.

"'You and I never set the place on fire,' he said gently, 'and there you are, we're not up in court, and we're not going to prison.'

"Both of them, husband and wife, tried to get me to eat and drink all they could. There were various little details – they way they brewed up the coffee together, for instance, or the fact that they understood one another almost without saying a word – which led me to conclude that they lived a peaceful and happy life together, and were pleased to have me as their guest. After dinner we played duets on the piano, then it grew dark and I went home. That was in early spring. After that I spent the whole summer at Sofyino without leaving, and I had no time to think about town; but the memory of that graceful fair-haired woman stayed with me day after day. I didn't think about her, but the light shadow of her seemed to rest on my heart.

"Late that autumn there was a charity performance of a play in town. I went up to the Governor's box (I'd been invited there in the interval) – and there was Anna Alexeyevna sitting next to the Governor's wife; and once again, that same irresistible, thrilling impression of her beauty and her lovely, gentle eyes, and again that same feeling of closeness.

"We sat side by side, and then walked about in the foyer.

"'You've lost weight,' she said. 'Have you been ill?'

"'Yes. I've got a frozen shoulder, and in wet weather I don't sleep well.'

"'You look out of sorts. Back in the springtime, when you came to dinner, you seemed younger and brighter. You got quite animated and talked a lot, very interestingly, and I must confess I was a bit carried away by you. During the summer, for some reason, you often came to my mind, and when I was getting ready for the theatre today, I had the feeling that I'd see you.'

"She laughed.

"'But today you're looking out of sorts,' she said again. 'That ages you.'

"Next day I had lunch with the Luganoviches. After lunch they set off for their house in the country, to get the place ready for winter, and I went with them. Then I came back to town with them, and at midnight we were drinking tea in a quiet family atmosphere by the fireside, while the young mother kept going out to see if her baby girl was asleep. After that, whenever I came to town, I always visited the Luganoviches. They got used to me, and I got used to going there. Generally I'd come in unannounced, like one of the family.

"'Who's there?' The words would come from a distant room, in the drawn-out voice I found so charming.

"'It's Pavel Konstantinich,' the maid or nursemaid would reply.

"Anna Alexeyevna would come out to greet me with an anxious face, and always asked me:

"'Why haven't you been for so long? Has anything happened?'

"The look she gave me, the refined, elegant hand she offered me, her indoor dress, her hairdo, her voice and her steps, always gave me the same feeling of something new, important and unusual in my life. We spent a long time talking and a long time saying nothing, each thinking their own thoughts, or else she might play the piano for me. If there was no one at home, I would wait and talk to the nurse, or play with the baby, or stretch out on the Turkish divan in the study to read the paper; and when Anna Alexeyevna came in, I would meet her in the hall and take all her parcels from her, and for some reason I always carried those parcels as solemnly and lovingly as if I were a little boy.

"As the proverb has it – the peasant's wife had no troubles in her life, so she bought herself a pig. The Luganoviches had no troubles, so they made friends with me. If I stayed away from town for a long while, that meant I was ill or something had happened to me, and they both got very anxious. They worried because I, an educated man who knew foreign languages and ought to have been occupying myself with science or literature, was living in the country, running round in circles like a squirrel on a wheel, working hard, and never having a penny. They thought that I was suffering; and that if I talked, laughed and ate, that was just to hide my suffering. Even at cheerful moments when I was happy, I could feel their questioning eyes on me. They were particularly touching when I really did pass through difficult times, when some creditor was pressing me or I didn't have enough money for an urgent payment. Then husband and wife would both go and whisper together by the window, and he would come to me with a serious expression and say:

"'Pavel Konstantinich, if you're short of money right now, my wife and I beg you not to hesitate to borrow some from us.'

"And his ears would blush red with emotion. Sometimes it happened that they would whisper together by the window like that, and then he would come to me, ears blushing red, and say:

"'My wife and I would be so glad if you'd accept this present from us.'

"And he'd give me a pair of cufflinks, or a cigarette case, or a lamp; and in return I'd send them a game bird, or butter, or flowers from the country. Incidentally, they were both very well off. Formerly I often used to borrow money, without being too particular about it – I'd get it wherever I could; but nothing on earth could ever have made me borrow from the Luganoviches. The very idea was out of the question.

"I was unhappy. In my house, in the fields, in the barn, I thought about her and tried to understand the mystery of a young, beautiful, intelligent woman who married a boring man, almost an old man (he was over forty), and had children by him – and to understand the mystery of that boring man, a good-hearted, simple fellow, who argued in such a boring, right-thinking way, and always stayed close to the solid people at balls and receptions; listless, useless, with a docile, detached expression, as if he'd been brought along for sale; but who still believed in his right to be happy, and to have children by her; and I kept trying to understand why she had to have met him first, instead of me, and why this dreadful mistake had to happen in our lives.

"When I came to town, I could always tell from her eyes that she'd been expecting me; and she herself would confess that right from early morning she'd had a sort of special feeling, and guessed that I would come. We spent a long time talking or saying nothing, but we didn't admit that we loved one another – timidly, jealously, we kept that secret. We were afraid of anything that might reveal our secret to ourselves. I loved her tenderly, deeply, but I thought about it, and wondered where our love could lead us if we didn't have the strength to fight it. I couldn't believe that this quiet, sad love of mine could suddenly destroy the happy lives of her husband, her children, and all that household where I was so much loved and trusted. Would that have been honourable? She would have gone away with me, but where to? Where could I have taken her? It would have been different if I had led a beautiful, interesting life, if I had been fighting for my country's freedom, say, or been a famous scientist, or performer, or artist – but as it was, I'd have been taking her from one ordinary, everyday way of life and leading her to another that was just the same, or even more ordinary. And how long would we have gone on being happy? What would happen to her if I fell ill, or died, or even if we just fell out of love?

"And she seemed to think the same way. She thought of her husband, her children, her mother who loved the husband like a son. If she had given way to her feelings, she would either have had to lie, or to tell the truth; and in

444444

her situation both would be equally terrible and awkward. She was tormented by the question of whether her love would bring me happiness, or would complicate my life which was difficult enough without that, and full of all sorts of troubles. She thought that she was no longer young enough for me, not hard-working or energetic enough to start a new life, and she often talked to her husband about how I needed to marry an intelligent, worthy girl who would be a good housewife and helper to me – and she'd immediately add that one could probably never find a girl like that in the whole town.

"Meanwhile the years passed. Anna Alexeyevna already had two children. When I visited the Luganoviches, the servants would give me welcoming smiles, the children would shout that Uncle Pavel Konstantinich had arrived, and hang about my neck – everybody was pleased. They had no idea what was going on in my heart, and thought that I was pleased too. Everybody regarded me as a man of honour. Adults and children all felt that this was a man of honour walking about the room, and that gave a special sort of charm to their relations with me, as if their lives too were made purer and finer by my presence. Anna Alexeyevna and I would go to the theatre together, always on foot; we would sit side by side in the stalls, shoulders touching; I would silently take the opera glasses from her hands, and at that point I would feel that she was close to me, that she was mine, that we couldn't live without one another; but by some strange misunderstanding, when we left the theatre we would say goodbye and part like strangers. Heaven knows what stories were being spread about us in town by that time, but there wasn't a word of truth in any of them.

"In later years Anna Alexeyevna took to going away more often, to visit her mother or sister; she became moody, often feeling that her life was blighted and unfulfilled, and that she didn't want to see her husband or children. She was already being treated for a nervous disorder.

"We kept not talking to one another, and when other people were around she felt a strange sort of irritation with me – no matter what I talked about, she'd disagree with me, and if I got into an argument, she'd side with my opponent. If I dropped anything, she'd say coldly:

"'Congratulations.'

"If I forgot the opera glasses when I took her to the theatre, later on she'd say:

"'I just knew you'd forget.'

"Fortunately or unfortunately, there's nothing in our lives that doesn't come to an end sooner or later. The time came when we had to part, because Luganovich was appointed chairman of the court in one of the western provinces. They had to sell their furniture, their horses and their house in the country. When they went there, and then looked around before returning home, so as to get a last glimpse of the garden and the green roof, everyone felt sad, and I realized that the time had come to say farewell to more than just that house. It was decided that at the end of August we would see Anna Alexeyevna off on her way to the Crimea, where her doctors were sending her, and a short while after that Luganovich and the children would set out for his western province.

"A great crowd of us came to see Anna Alexeyevna off. After she had said goodbye to her husband and children, and there was only a moment left before the third bell, I ran into her compartment to put one of her baskets up onto the rack – she had almost forgotten it; and we had to part. When our eyes met, there in the railway compartment, our spiritual strength failed us both. I embraced her, she pressed her face against my breast, and our eyes filled with tears; as I kissed her face, shoulders and arms, wet with tears – oh, how unhappy we both were! – I told her I loved her, and with a burning pain in my heart I realized how unnecessary, trivial and false everything had been that prevented us from loving one another. I realized that when you are in love, you must start your reflections about your love with what is highest, what is more important than happiness or unhappiness, or sin or virtue in their accepted senses – or you shouldn't reflect at all.

"I kissed her for the last time, squeezed her hand, and we parted for ever. The train had already started. I sat down in the next compartment – it was empty – and remained sitting there and weeping until the next station. Then I made my way back home to Sofyino on foot…"

While Aliokhin was telling his story, the rain had stopped and the sun had peeped through. Burkin and Ivan Ivanich stepped out onto the veranda, which had a beautiful view over the garden and a stretch of river, now gleaming like a mirror in the sunlight. They admired the view and felt sorry for this man with his kind, intelligent eyes, who had told them his story so openheartedly, and who really was running round and round like a squirrel on a wheel, on this huge estate, instead of devoting himself to science or something else that could have brightened his life. And they thought how grief-stricken that young woman must have looked, when he parted from her in the railway compartment and kissed her face and shoulders. They had both met her in town, and Burkin actually knew her and found her beautiful.

# GRIEF

G RIGORY PETROV the turner, long known as an outstanding master of his trade, and also as the most feckless peasant in the whole of Galchino district, is driving his sick old woman to the hospital. He has to cover over twenty miles, along a dreadful road – a government post driver could never have managed it, let alone a layabout like Grigory the turner. There's a biting cold wind blowing in his face. Wherever he looks, great clouds of snowflakes are eddying about, so that there's no telling whether it's snowing from the sky or the ground. The driving snow makes it impossible to see the fields, or the telegraph poles, or the forest, and when a particularly strong gust of wind blows in his face, he can't even make out the yoke over the horse's neck. The feeble, worn-out little mare can barely manage to drag herself along. All her energy is used up in pulling her hooves out of the deep snow, and tugging with her head. The turner is in a hurry, bouncing restlessly up and down on the front seat and continually whipping his horse on the back.

"Don't you worry, Matryona…" he mumbles. "Put up with it for a bit. We'll get to the hospital, God willing, and you'll be all right in a jiffy… Pavel Ivanich will give you some drops, or he'll have you bled, or maybe his Honour will want you rubbed down with spirit or something, and that'll be… it'll draw it out of your side. Pavel Ivanich will do his best… He'll shout at you, and stamp his feet a bit, but he'll do what he can… A lovely man, so caring, God grant him health… In a minute, when we get there, the first thing he'll do, he'll come running out of his quarters and start calling down all the devils. 'What's this? What's the meaning of it?' he'll shout. 'Why didn't you get here in time? What am I, a dog or something, wasting my time fussing over you devils all day? Why didn't you come this morning? Get out! Out of here this instant! Come back tomorrow!' – And I'll say: 'Mr Doctor, sir! Pavel Ivanich! Your Excellency!' Will you get on, confound you, you devil! Giddy-up!"

The turner whips up his little mare, and without looking at his old woman, goes on muttering to himself:

"'Your Excellency! As true as God's my witness… see this cross… I left as soon as it was light. How could I have got here in time, if the Lord… Mother of God… in his anger, sent down a blizzard like this? You can see for yourself… Even the best horse couldn't have got through, and mine, see for yourself, she isn't a horse but a disgrace!' – And Pavel Ivanich will give a scowl and shout 'I know your sort! Always ready with an excuse! Specially you, Grishka! I've known you a long time! You'll have stopped at a tavern half a dozen times on your way!' – And I'll tell him, 'Your Excellency! What do you take me for? A wicked man, or a heathen? Here's my old woman giving up her soul to God, she's dying, and I'm supposed to be going to taverns! Do you mind! To hell with all those taverns!' – And then Pavel Ivanich will get you carried down to the hospital. And I'll fall down at his feet: 'Pavel Ivanich! Your Excellency! Thank you most humbly! Forgive us in our ignorance, cursed sinners that we are, don't blame us simple peasants! We deserve to be thrown out on our ears, but you're being kind enough to help us, and getting your feet wet in the snow!' – And Pavel Ivanich will give me a look, as if he was going to hit me, and he'll say, 'Instead of flopping down at my feet, you fool, you'd do better to give up swilling vodka and look after your old lady. You deserve a good thrashing!' – 'Yes indeed, a thrashing, Pavel Ivanich, God strike me, a thrashing! But how can I help bowing down to your feet, when you're our benefactor, our own father? Your Excellency! I tell you honestly... before God... spit in my eyes if I'm telling a lie: just as soon as my Matryona, that's it... as soon as she's well again, and back in her rightful place, then I'll do anything for your Honour, anything you ask! A little cigar box, if you want, from Karelian birch... croquet balls... I could turn you some skittles, just like the foreign kind... I'll do anything for you! I won't take a kopek off you! A cigar box like that would set you back four roubles in Moscow, but I won't take a kopek!' – And the doctor will laugh, and say 'That'll do, that'll do… I'm sorry for you! Only it's a shame you're a drunkard…' – You see, old woman, I know how to talk to gentry folk. There isn't a gentleman alive that I wouldn't know how to talk to. If only God doesn't let us lose the road. What a snowstorm! I can't see a thing any more."

The turner goes on chattering non-stop. It's his tongue that's chattering mechanically, just to blank out his misery a little. He has plenty of words on his tongue, and even more thoughts and questions in his head. Grief has come upon him without any warning, unexpected and unsuspected, and now he's trying in vain to pull himself together, recover himself, make sense of it all. Up till now he's lived a calm, untroubled life, in a drunken semi-oblivion, knowing neither grief nor joy; and now suddenly a terrible pain has entered his soul. This carefree layabout and small-time drunkard now finds himself suddenly a busy man, full of anxieties, racing against time and even battling with the forces of nature.

The turner remembers that all this trouble began the evening before. When he returned home last night, tipsy as always, and started cursing and flailing his fists about as he usually did, the old woman had looked at her ruffian in a way she had never done before. Usually her eyes would have had the look of a martyr – the meek look of a dog used to being beaten regularly and half-starved; but now her look was stern and fixed, like a painted saint on an icon, or a dying person. All his grief had come from those strange, unfriendly eyes. The stupefied turner had begged his neighbour for his little mare, and now he was driving the old woman to hospital in the hope that Pavel Ivanich and his powders and ointments would give his wife her old look again.

"Look here, Matryona, I mean…" he mumbles. "If Pavel Ivanich asks you whether I used to beat you or not, you tell him I never did! And I won't beat you any more. I swear on the cross. Anyway, did I ever beat you because I was angry? I just beat you like that, for no reason. I'm fond of you. Another man wouldn't care, but here I am, driving you… doing my best. But what a blizzard! Lord, Thy will be done! So long as God doesn't let us lose our way… Is your side hurting you, then? Matryona, why don't you say anything? I'm asking you, is your side hurting you?"

It strikes him as odd that the snow doesn't melt on the old woman's face, and odd that her face itself looks somehow drawn out, and has turned a pale grey colour like dirty wax, and is looking stern and serious.

"You old fool!" mutters the turner. "I'm talking to you straight, as God's my witness… and you just… You fool! I've a good mind not to take you to Pavel Ivanich after all!"

He drops the reins and starts thinking. He daren't turn round and look at the old woman – it's too frightening. Asking her a question and getting no answer is frightening too. Eventually, to settle his doubts without looking round at his wife, he feels for her cold hand and lifts it up. It falls back like a length of rope.

"Must have died, then! What a business!"

The turner begins to weep. Not that he's so sorry, rather he's vexed. He thinks to himself: how quickly everything happens in this world! No sooner has his grief begun than it's all done. He's never managed to live with his old woman, and tell her everything, and be nice to her, and now she's died. He lived with her for forty years, but then those forty years all went by in a sort of fog. What with his drunkenness, and the fights, and their poverty, he's never felt his life. And now, as if to spite him, the old woman has died just at the moment when he's feeling fond of her, and that he can't live without her, and that he's treated her terribly badly.

"And she used to go all round the village!" he remembers. "I used to send her out myself, begging people for bread – what a business! The silly fool, she ought to have lived another ten years; as it is, she probably thinks that's what I'm really like. Holy Mother of God, where the devil am I driving? No point getting her treated now, she's got to be buried. Turn about!"

He turns the sledge round and whips up the horse with all his might. The driving gets worse hour by hour. Now he can't even see the yoke. Sometimes the sledge rides up onto a young fir tree; a dark shape scrapes against his hands, flashes before his eyes, and then there's nothing before his eyes again but whirling white snow.

"If I could have my life over again…" he thinks.

He thinks back to forty-odd years ago, when Matryona was young and beautiful, a merry lass from a well-to-do family. They had married her to him because they admired his craftsmanship. The two of them would have had all they needed for a good life; the trouble was that he had got drunk straight after the wedding, collapsed onto the stove, and seemed never to have awoken since that time. He remembers the wedding; but what happened after that – he can't remember for the life of him. Except that he got drunk, and lay around, and got into fights. And forty years had gone up in smoke, just like that.

Now the white snow clouds are slowly beginning to turn grey. Dusk is falling.

"Where am I going?" the turner suddenly thinks with a start. "I have to bury her, not take her to hospital… I think I've gone mad!"

He turns back once more, and lashes his horse again. The little mare strains its hardest, and snorts, and sets off at a little trot. Over and over again, he whips her on her back… He can hear something knocking behind him, and although he doesn't look back, he knows that the dead woman's head is banging against the sledge. The air grows darker and darker, and the wind blows sharper and colder...

"If I could have my life again..." thinks the turner. "I'd get a new lathe, take orders... hand the money over to my wife... yes!"

But now he drops the reins. He hunts for them, wants to take them up again, but can't manage – his hands don't work...

"Never mind..." he thinks. "The horse will get there on its own – it knows the way. If I could sleep a bit now... Before the funeral, or the requiem, it'd be nice to lie down."

The turner shuts his eyes and falls into a doze. A little later, he can hear the horse stopping. He opens his eyes and sees something dark ahead, something like a hut or a haystack...

He ought to get down from the sledge and find out what's going on, but his whole body feels so lazy that he'd rather freeze to death than move from the spot... And he falls into a peaceful sleep.

He wakes in a large room with painted walls. Bright sunlight is flooding through the windows. He can see people around him, and the first thing he wants to do is show that he's a respectable man who knows what's what.

"We have to arrange a requiem, brothers, for my old woman!" he says. "The priest has to be told..."

"That'll do, that'll do! You lie back down!" someone interrupts him.

"Heavens! Pavel Ivanich!" exclaims the turner in amazement, seeing the doctor in front of him. "Yerexlency! My benefactor!"

He wants to leap up and get down on the floor before this representative of medicine, but he can feel that his arms and legs aren't obeying him.

"Your Excellency! Where are my legs? And my arms?"

"Say goodbye to your arms and legs... Frozen off! Now, now, what are you crying about? You've had your life, and thank God for that! I expect you've clocked up sixty and more – what more do you want?"

"That's terrible!... Your Excellency, it's terrible! Please, please forgive me! Another five or six years..."

"What for?"

"The horse isn't mine, I have to give it back... And bury my old woman... And how quickly everything happens on this earth! Your Excellency! Pavel Ivanich! A little cigar box, finest Karelian birch! I'll turn you a little croquet set..."

The doctor waves his hand and leaves the ward. That turner – amen, he's done for!

# THE BET

I T WAS A DARK AUTUMN NIGHT. The old banker paced back and forth in his study, remembering a party he had given one autumn evening fifteen years ago. There had been many clever people there, and interesting conversations. One of the topics had been the death penalty. Most of the guests, who had included quite a number of intellectuals and journalists, disapproved of the death penalty, calling it an outdated and immoral method of punishment, unworthy of a Christian state. Some of them took the view that wherever the death penalty existed, it ought to be replaced by life imprisonment.

"I don't agree with you," said their host the banker. "I haven't experienced either capital punishment or life imprisonment, but if one can judge *a priori*, I believe that execution is more ethical and humane than imprisonment. Execution kills a man at once, while life imprisonment kills him slowly. So which executioner is more humane? The one who kills you over a few minutes, or the one who drags the life out of you for years on end?"

"Both are equally immoral," commented one of the guests, "because they each have the same aim – to take away your life. The state isn't God. It has no right to take away something it can't give back if it wants to."

One of the guests was a lawyer, a young man of about twenty-five. When asked his opinion, he said:

"Capital punishment and life imprisonment are equally immoral, but if I were asked to choose between the two, naturally I'd choose the second. Living somehow or other is better than not living at all."

A lively argument followed. The banker, who had been younger and more excitable at the time, suddenly lost his self-possession, thumped his fist on the table, and shouted at the young lawyer:

"Not true! I bet you two million you won't even last out five years in solitary!"

"If you're serious," replied the lawyer, "I bet you I'll last out fifteen years, not five."

"Fifteen? Done!" cried the banker. "Gentlemen, I'm staking two million!"

"Agreed! You stake your millions, and I'll stake my freedom!" said the lawyer.

And that crazy, senseless wager was actually concluded! The banker, a spoilt and frivolous man, with uncounted millions at the time, was thrilled with his bet. At dinner he made fun of the lawyer, telling him:

"Think again, young man, before it's too late. Two

million means nothing to me, but you're risking three or four of the best years of your life. I say three or four, because you won't stand it longer than that. And then, don't forget, you poor thing, that voluntary imprisonment is far harder to bear than when it's compulsory. The thought that you could walk free any minute will poison your entire existence in your cell. I pity you!"

And now the banker, as he paced back and forth, remembered all this and asked himself:

"What was the point of that bet? What's the use of the lawyer wasting fifteen years of his life, while I throw away two million? Will that prove to anyone whether capital punishment is worse or better than life imprisonment? No, and no again. It's all pointless nonsense. On my part, that was the whim of a well-fed man, and on the lawyer's part, nothing but greed for money…"

And he went on to remember what had happened after that party. It was decided that the lawyer would sit out his confinement under the strictest supervision in one of the outbuildings situated in the banker's garden. They agreed that for fifteen years he would be denied the right to cross the threshold of that building, or see any living person, or hear a human voice, or receive letters and newspapers. He was allowed to have a musical instrument, to read books, write letters, drink wine and smoke tobacco. His only contact with the outside world, under the agreed conditions, was to be in silence, through a little window built for the purpose.

ANTON CHEKHOV

He could receive anything he needed – books, music, wine and the rest – on a written request, in any quantity he liked, but only through that window. The agreement covered every last little detail that would ensure that his confinement was strictly solitary, and compelled the lawyer to serve *exactly* fifteen years, starting at 12 o'clock on 14th November 1870, and ending at 12 o'clock on 14th November 1885. The slightest attempt on his part to break the conditions, even two minutes before the agreed term, would release the banker from the obligation to pay him the two million.

During the first year of his confinement, the lawyer (as far as could be judged from his brief notes) suffered severe loneliness and boredom. Day and night, the sounds of the piano were constantly heard from his lodge. He gave up wine and tobacco. Wine, he wrote, arouses longings, and longings are the prisoner's greatest enemy; besides, there was nothing more dreary than drinking good wine without seeing anyone. And tobacco spoiled the air in his room. During his first year, the lawyer was mostly sent light literature – novels with a complicated love plot, detective stories, tales of fantasy, comedies and the like.

During his second year, the music in his house fell silent, and in his notes the lawyer asked for nothing but classics. In his fifth year, music was heard once more, and the prisoner asked for wine. The people who watched him through his window said that he had spent the whole of that year just eating, drinking and lying on his bed, often yawning, and talking angrily to himself. He read no books. Sometimes at night he would sit down to write; he would spend hours writing, and then when morning came tear up everything he had written. More than once he was heard crying.

In the second half of his sixth year, the prisoner began intensively studying languages, philosophy and history. He threw himself into these studies so passionately that the banker could scarcely keep up with his demands for books. Over the course of four years, some six hundred volumes were obtained at his request. It was during this phase of his activities that the banker received the following letter from his prisoner:

"Dear Jailer! I am writing these lines to you in six languages. Show them to the following people, and have them read them. If they fail to find a single mistake in them, I beg you to order a gun to be fired in the garden. That shot will tell me that my efforts have not been wasted. Geniuses of every age and land have spoken in different languages, but they all have one and the same flame burning within them. O, if you only knew what sublime happiness my soul enjoys, now that I can understand them!"

The prisoner's wish was granted. The banker ordered two shots to be fired in the garden.

Later on, after his tenth year, the lawyer sat motionless at his desk reading nothing but the Gospels. It seemed strange to the banker that a man who had mastered six hundred learned volumes over the course of four years should now spend almost a year reading a single book that was neither thick nor hard to understand. The Gospels were followed by religious history and theology.

During the last two years of his confinement, the prisoner read great quantities, quite indiscriminately. He would take up natural science, and then demand Byron or Shakespeare. Some of the notes he sent asked for chemistry, and a medical textbook, and a novel, and some treatise of philosophy or theology, all at the same time. He read like a man afloat on the sea, surrounded by the wreckage of his ship, trying to save his life by desperately clutching first to one fragment and then another.

## I I

The old banker remembered all this and thought:

"Tomorrow at twelve, he'll get his freedom. Under the contract, I shall have to pay him two million. If I pay that, I'm done for – I shall be utterly ruined."

Fifteen years ago he could not count his millions; but today he feared to ask himself which was greater, his wealth or his debts. Playing the stock exchange, risky speculations, and the impetuousness which he couldn't shake off even in his old age, had gradually brought about the decline of his fortunes, and the fearless, self-confident, proud millionaire had turned into a middle-of-the-road banker who trembled at every rise and fall of his investments.

"That damned bet!" muttered the old man, clutching his head in despair. "Why didn't that man die? He's still only forty. He'll take my last penny, get married, enjoy his life, play the stock exchange, while I look on like an envious beggar, hearing the same words from him day after day: 'I owe you all my happiness, let me help you!' No, that's too much! My only way out of bankruptcy and disgrace is that man's death!"

The clock struck three. The banker listened: everyone in the house was asleep, and the only sound to be heard was the rustling of the cold trees outside the windows. Careful not to make a sound, he opened the fireproof safe and got out the key of the door that had not been opened for fifteen years. Then he put on his coat and went out.

The garden was dark and cold. It was raining. The damp, piercing wind blew howling through the garden, giving the trees no rest. The banker strained his eyes but could not make out either the ground, or the white statues, or the outbuilding, or the trees. When he reached the place where the outbuilding stood, he twice called out to the watchman. There was no reply. Evidently the watchman had taken shelter from the storm and was now asleep somewhere in the kitchen or the greenhouse.

"If I'm brave enough to do what I mean to," thought the old man, "then the first to be suspected will be the watchman."

He felt in the darkness for the steps and the door, and entered the hallway of the building. Then he groped his way into the little passage and lit a match. Not a soul was there. There was somebody's bedstead with no bedding on it, and in the corner the dark shape of a cast iron stove. The seals on the door to the prisoner's room were intact.

When his match went out, the old man, trembling with agitation, peered through the little window.

A candle was burning in the prisoner's room, giving a dim light. He was sitting at his table. All that could be seen was his back, the hair on his head, and his hands. Open books were lying about on the table, the two armchairs and the carpet by the table.

Five minutes passed without the prisoner once stirring. Fifteen years of confinement had taught him to sit very still. The banker tapped his finger on the window, but the prisoner did not move an inch. Then the banker carefully pulled off the seals from the door and inserted the key into the keyhole. The rusty lock made a grating sound and the door creaked. The banker expected to hear an instant cry of surprise and the sound of footsteps, but some three minutes passed and everything within remained as quiet as ever. He made up his mind to enter the room.

A man sat motionless at the table, a man unlike ordinary men. He was a skeleton, with the skin stretched over his bones, long feminine locks and an unkempt beard. His face was yellow with an earthy tint, his cheeks sunken, his back long and narrow, and the arm supporting his shaggy head was so thin and gaunt that it was dreadful to look at.

He already had a silvery sheen of grey hair on his head, and no one who saw his aged, emaciated face would have believed that he was only forty years old. He was asleep… In front of his bowed head, a sheet of paper covered in tiny writing lay on the table.

"What a sorry creature!" thought the banker. "He's sleeping, probably dreaming of his millions! And yet all I need do is take his half-dead body and throw him on the bed, stifle him a bit with a pillow, and the most conscientious of experts would never find any sign of a violent death. But first let's read what he's written here."

The banker picked up the paper from the table and read as follows:

"Tomorrow at twelve o'clock I receive my freedom and the right to associate with other people. But before leaving this room and seeing the sun, I have to write you a few words. In all conscience, as God is my witness, I declare to you that I despise both freedom, and life, and health, and all that your books call the good things of the world.

"For fifteen years, I have been intently studying earthly life. True, I saw neither the earth nor any people, but in your books I have drunk fragrant wine, sung songs, hunted deer and wild boar in the forests, loved women… Beauties, ethereal as clouds, created by the magic of your inspired poets, have visited me at night and whispered marvellous tales to me, leaving me drunk with wonder. In your books I have climbed the peaks of Elborus and Mont Blanc, and from there I have watched the sun rise in the mornings, and flood the sky, the ocean and the mountain tops with crimson and gold in the evenings. There, too, I have seen lightning flash as though above my very head, cleaving the storm clouds; I have seen green forests, fields, rivers, lakes, cities; I have heard the singing of sirens and the strains of shepherds' pipes, I have felt the wings of splendid devils who flew down to me to converse about God... In your books I have hurled myself into bottomless chasms, worked miracles, killed, burnt cities, preached new religions, conquered whole kingdoms...

"Your books have given me wisdom. All that the tireless human mind has created over the centuries is compressed in a small volume within my skull. I know that I am wiser than you all.

"And I despise your books, I despise all the good things and all the wisdom of the world. All is worthless, fleeting, illusory, deceptive as a mirage. You may all be proud, wise and beautiful, but death will wipe you off the face of the earth like the mice below your floors, and your posterity, your history, the immortal memory of your geniuses, will freeze or burn along with the earthly globe.

"You have lost your reason and are following the wrong path. You take lies for truth and ugliness for beauty. You would be astonished if circumstances caused frogs and lizards to grow on apple trees and orange trees, instead of their proper fruits; or if roses gave off the smell of a sweating horse; and so too I am astonished at you, who have exchanged heaven for earth. I do not wish to understand you.

"To prove to you in practice how I despise all you live for, I renounce the two millions that I once dreamed of as a paradise, and which I now scorn. In order to deprive myself of any right to them, I shall walk out of here five hours before the agreed term, and thereby break the compact…"

After reading this, the banker laid the paper on the table, kissed the strange man on the head, and wept; then he left the building. Never before, not even after heavy losses on the stock exchange, had he felt such contempt for himself as now. When he returned to his house, he lay down on his bed, but his agitation and tears kept him from sleep for a long time…

Next morning the white-faced watchmen ran in to tell him that they had seen the man who lived in the lodge climb out of his window into the garden, walk to the gates, and disappear. The banker immediately went over to the lodge with his servants and made sure that the prisoner had fled. To avoid unnecessary talk, he picked up the letter of renunciation from the table, returned home and locked it away in his fireproof safe.

# A MISFORTUNE

SOFIA PETROVNA, Lubyantsev the notary's wife, a good-looking young woman of twenty-five, was walking slowly along a forest track with Ilyin, a lawyer staying at a nearby lodge. It was a little after four in the afternoon. Fluffy white clouds had gathered above the track, with a few patches of bright blue sky peeping between them. The clouds hung motionless, as if caught on the tops of the tall old pines. The air was still and heavy.

In the distance the forest cutting was crossed by a low railway embankment where, just then, a sentry with a gun was pacing up and down for some reason. Just beyond the embankment a large white church could be seen, with six domes and a rusty roof.

"I wasn't expecting to meet you here," said Sofia Petrovna, looking down at the ground and prodding last year's leaves with the tip of her umbrella. "But now I'm glad we've met. I need to have a serious talk to you, once and for all. Please, Ivan Mikhailovich, if you really love and respect me, then stop following me! You stick to me like a shadow, you're always looking at me in a way that you shouldn't, you declare you're in love with me, you write me peculiar letters and… and I've no idea how all this is going to end! I mean, good God, what's it all leading to?"

Ilyin said nothing. Sofia Petrovna walked on a few steps, and continued:

"You've suddenly changed, over two or three weeks, after we've known each other for five years. I don't recognize you, Ivan Mikhailovich!"

Sofia Petrovna stole a sideways glance at her companion. He had screwed up his eyes and was looking hard at the fluffy clouds. His face was angry, sulky and preoccupied, like a man in anguish who is being forced to listen to nonsense.

"I'm surprised you can't understand that yourself!" went on Lubyantseva, shrugging her shoulders. "You must see this game you've started playing with me isn't a pretty one. I'm married, I love and respect my husband… I have a daughter… Don't you care about any of that? Besides which – you're a very old friend, you know my feelings about family life… what holds a marriage together…"

Ilyin grunted crossly and sighed.

"Holds a marriage together…" he muttered. "O God!"

"Yes, yes… I love my husband, I respect him, and in any event I value our peaceful family life. I'd sooner let myself be killed than bring misery on Andrey and his daughter… So I beg you, Ivan Mikhailovich, in God's name, leave me in peace. Let's be good and kind friends again as we used to be, and please leave off all this sighing and lamenting – it doesn't suit you. There now, that's that! Not another word. Let's talk about something different."

Sofia Petrovna gave Ilyin another sidelong look. He was staring upwards, his face was pale, and he was angrily biting his trembling lips. Lubyantseva couldn't understand why he was cross or what was making him so indignant, but she was troubled by his pallor.

"Come on, don't be cross. Let's be friends..." she said gently. "All right? Here's my hand."

Ilyin took her plump little hand in both of his, squeezed it and slowly raised it to his lips.

"I'm not a schoolboy," he muttered. "I'm not in the least interested in being friends with the woman I love."

"Stop it, stop it! That's decided and settled! Now we've got to this bench, let's sit down..."

A delicious sense of relief filled Sofia Petrovna's heart. The most difficult and delicate part of what she needed to say had been said. The agonizing problem was dealt with and settled. Now at last she could take a deep breath in peace, and look Ilyin in the face. She looked at him, and was pleasantly flattered by the selfish feeling of superiority a beloved woman has over the man who loves her. She enjoyed seeing this huge, powerful man, with his angry, manly face and big black beard – intelligent, cultured, and, people said, talented – sit down obediently beside her and bow his head. They sat in silence for two or three minutes.

"Nothing's decided, and nothing's finished with…" began Ilyin. "You sound as if you're reciting words out of a schoolbook – 'I love and respect my husband… what holds a marriage together…' I know all that without you telling me, and I could go further. I tell you, honestly and truly, that I regard my behaviour as immoral and criminal. But where does that get us? What's the point of saying what everybody already knows? Instead of feeding a nightingale with useless words, you'd better tell me what I'm to do."

"I've already told you: you have to leave!"

"I've already left five times over, as you know perfectly well – and every time I turned back halfway! I can show you my express railway tickets; I've kept them all. I haven't got the will to run away from you. I fight against it, I fight like mad, but what the devil am I good for, if I don't have the backbone, if I'm a coward and a weakling! I can't fight against nature! Do you understand? I can't! I run away, and nature pulls me back by my coat-tails. It's a shameful, loathsome weakness!"

Ilyin flushed, stood up and started pacing back and forth near the bench.

"I'm as furious as a dog!" he growled, clenching both fists. "I hate myself, I despise myself! My God, I'm like a perverted schoolboy, trailing around after another man's wife, writing idiotic letters, humiliating myself… Ugh!"

Ilyin clutched his head, grunted and sat down again.

"And then, you're so insincere!" he went on bitterly. "If you don't like the ugly game I'm playing, why did you come here today? What made you come? All I've asked you for in my letters is a straight, final answer – yes or no. But instead of giving me a straight answer, you just contrive to meet me 'accidentally' day after day, and then treat me to quotations out of school textbooks!"

Lubyantseva was startled, and blushed. She suddenly felt the same awkwardness that a respectable woman feels when someone catches her undressed.

"You seem to suspect me of playing a game…" she said uncertainly. "I've always given you straight answers, and… and today I was begging you!"

"Oh, what's the good of begging in a situation like this? If you'd told me straight off, 'Go away!', I'd have been gone long ago; but you never said that. Not a single time have you given me a straight answer. Strangely indecisive of you! Honest to God, either you're playing a game with me, or else…"

Ilyin broke off, and rested his head on his clenched fists. Sofia Petrovna cast her mind back to her behaviour from the very first, until now. She remembered that she had resisted Ilyin's courtship right from the start, not only in her deeds but even in her innermost thoughts; and yet at the same time she felt that there was some truth in what the lawyer said. She didn't know exactly what that truth was, and try as she might, she couldn't work out how to answer Ilyin's accusations. Saying nothing was awkward, so she shrugged her shoulders and said:

"So it's my fault, then."

"I'm not blaming you for being insincere," sighed Ilyin. "That just came out... Your insincerity is natural and inevitable. If everyone got together and agreed to talk sincerely all at once, everything would simply fall apart."

Sofia Petrovna was in no mood for philosophy, but glad of a chance to change the subject.

"Why is that?" she asked.

"Because the only creatures that are sincere are savages and animals. With the advent of civilization, we have come to need certain comforts in our lives, including virtue in women; and that makes sincerity impossible."

Ilyin angrily poked his stick into the sand. Lubyantseva listened to him without understanding much of what he said, but she liked his conversation. What she liked most of all was the fact that she, an ordinary woman, had a talented man talking to her about "clever subjects". What was more, she was getting great pleasure from watching the movements of his pale, lively and still angry young face. There was a lot that she didn't understand, but she could clearly see the attraction of this modern man so boldly settling important questions and drawing definitive conclusions, with no doubts or hesitation.

She suddenly realized that she was looking admiringly at him, and took fright.

"Excuse me, but I don't understand," she said hurriedly. "Why did you start talking about insincerity? Let me ask you again, please – will you be a dear, kind friend and leave me in peace? I'm asking you in all sincerity!"

"All right. I'll go on fighting with myself!" sighed Ilyin. "My pleasure, I'll do my best… Only I doubt if all that fighting will do any good. I'll either put a bullet in my brain, or… I'll be really stupid and take to drink. There's no hope for me! Everything has its limits, and fighting against nature does too. Tell me, how can one fight against madness? If you drink wine, how can you beat your intoxication? What can I do, if the image of you has grown into my very soul, so that it stands just as inexorably before my eyes as this pine tree here? Please, teach me – what exploit do I have to perform, to free myself from my abject, miserable condition, when all my thoughts, all my desires and dreams, belong not to me, but to some kind of demon that's settled inside me? I love you, I love you so much that I've lost my way, given up my work and my friends, and forgotten my God! Never in my life have I loved like this!"

Sofia Petrovna, who hadn't expected this sudden outburst, drew back bodily from Ilyin and looked fearfully into his face. There were tears in his eyes now, his lips were trembling, and his whole face was bathed in a hungry, imploring expression.

"I love you!" he muttered, bringing his eyes closer to her large, frightened eyes. "You're so lovely! I'm suffering now, but I swear to you, I could spend my whole life like this, sitting and suffering and looking into your eyes. Only… don't speak, I implore you!"

Sofia Petrovna seemed to be taken by surprise; she was hurriedly trying to think of some words to stop Ilyin. "I'll go away!" she decided, but before she could make any move to stand up, Ilyin was already kneeling at her feet… He was hugging her knees, gazing up at her face, and talking earnestly, passionately, beautifully. In her terror and confusion she did not hear what he was saying. Now, for some reason, at this dangerous moment, when her knees were being pleasantly held as though in a warm bath, she experienced a kind of wicked pleasure as she searched for some meaning in what she felt. She was angry at finding herself filled through and through not with virtuous protestations, but with helplessness, laziness and emptiness, like a drunken man who's beyond caring. Only in the very depths of her soul was there a faraway part of her that malignantly taunted her: "Why don't you walk away? This is how it has to be, then? Is that it?"

Searching for some sense in it all, she couldn't understand why she hadn't pulled away her hand, to which Ilyin had attached himself like a leech; or why she had hurriedly looked to the right and left, at the same moment as Ilyin, to see if anybody was watching. The pines and the clouds stood motionless, looking sternly down at them like old school ushers watching the pupils misbehaving, but bribed not to tell the authorities. The sentry stood on his embankment, stiff as a post, and seemed to be looking at the bench.

"Let him look!" thought Sofia Petrovna.

"But... but listen!" she finally brought out in desperation. "Where's all this going to lead? What's going to happen next?"

"I don't know! I don't know..." he whispered, waving aside her awkward questions.

There came the wheezy, tremulous whistle of a locomotive. That cold, irrelevant sound from the prosaic everyday world gave Lubyantseva a start.

"I have to hurry... I must go!" she said, and hastily stood up. "The train's coming... Andrey will be here! He has to have his dinner."

Sofia Petrovna turned her burning face towards the embankment. First the locomotive crawled slowly past, and then the wagons. It was not the local passenger train, as Lubyantseva had thought, but a goods train. A long procession of wagons, following one after another like the days of a man's life, rolled past against the white background of the church; and there seemed to be no end to them!

But finally the train had passed, and the last wagon with its lights and its guard vanished in the greenery. Sofia Petrovna abruptly turned away, and without looking at Ilyin, walked quickly off down the forest cutting. She was in control of herself again. Red-faced with shame, offended not by Ilyin, no, but by her own cowardice, and by the shameless way that she, a chaste and virtuous woman, had allowed a man who was not her husband to embrace her knees. She had only one thought now – how to get back to her home and family as quickly as possible. The lawyer could scarcely keep up with her. When she turned off the forest cutting onto a narrow path, she glanced back at him so quickly that all she saw was the sand on his knees. She gestured at him to drop back.

She ran the rest of the way home and then stood motionless in her room for five minutes, gazing now at the window, now at her writing table…

"You vicious creature!" she upbraided herself. "You vicious creature!"

She tormented herself by recalling, in every detail, how for all these days she had objected to Ilyin's lovemaking, and yet had been *drawn* to seek out a heart-to-heart talk with him. Worse still, when he was on the ground at her feet, she had enjoyed it enormously. She remembered it all, spared herself nothing, and now, breathless with shame, she would have been glad to slap herself in the face.

"Poor Andrey," she thought, and in recalling her husband she tried to give his face as tender an expression as she could. "Varya, my poor little girl, doesn't know what sort of a mother she has! Forgive me, my darlings! I love you both… very, very much!"

Wishing to prove to herself that she was still a good wife and mother, and that the corruption hadn't yet extended to the things that "hold a marriage together", as she had put it to Ilyin, Sofia Petrovna ran into the kitchen and shouted at the cook for not having yet laid the table for Andrey Ilyich. She tried to imagine her husband's exhausted, famished look, said aloud how sorry she felt for him, and personally laid the table for him, which she had never done before. Then she found her daughter Varya, lifted her up and gave her a big hug. The girl seemed heavy and indifferent, but her mother tried not to admit that to herself, and began explaining to the child what a good, kind and honourable papa she had.

On the other hand, when Andrey Ilyich arrived home, she barely greeted him. Her rush of contrived emotions had already passed, without changing her mind in any way, but merely irritating and annoying her with its falsehood. She was sitting by the window, miserable and angry. Only when misfortune strikes do people realize how hard it is to be master of one's own feelings and thoughts. Later on Sofia Petrovna would explain that she was in "the sort of muddle that was as hard to sort out as to count a flock of sparrows flying around". For instance, the fact that she wasn't pleased to see her husband arrive, and didn't like the way he behaved at table, suddenly led her to conclude that she was beginning to hate him.

Andrey Ilyich, weary from hunger and fatigue, flung himself on a plate of cold sausage while waiting for his soup to be served, and ate it greedily, munching noisily and moving his temples.

"My God," thought Sofia Petrovna, "I love him and respect him, but… why does he have to chew so disgustingly?"

Her thoughts were as confused as her emotions. Like anyone unaccustomed to struggling with unpleasant thoughts, Lubyantseva was trying with all her might not to think about her trouble, and the harder she tried, the more vividly Ilyin stood out in her imagination, with the sand on his knees, and the fluffy clouds, and the train…

"Why was I such a fool as to go out today?" she tormented herself. "Am I really the sort of person who can't trust herself?"

Fear makes everything seem bigger. By the time Andrey Ilyich was finishing his final course, she had firmly made up her mind to tell her husband everything, and escape the danger!

"Andrey, I have to have a serious talk with you," she began after dinner, when her husband was taking off his coat and boots to lie down for a rest.

"Well?"

"Let's go away from here!"

"Hmm… where to? It's too soon to go back to town."

"No, let's go on a journey, or something like that…"

"A journey…" muttered the notary, stretching his limbs. "I'd been dreaming of that myself – but where would we get the money, and whom could I leave in charge of the office?"

He thought a bit, and added:

A MISFORTUNE

"You're right, you're bored here. Go off by yourself, if you like!"

Sofia Petrovna agreed, but then realized at once that Ilyin would leap at his chance and go with her, on the same train, in the same carriage... She thought about it and looked at her husband, satisfied now he had eaten, but still weary. For some reason she found herself looking at his feet, small and almost feminine, in striped socks: each sock had a little thread sticking up from the toe...

Behind the lowered blind, a bumblebee was buzzing and knocking against the glass. Sofia Petrovna looked at the threads, listened to the bumblebee, and imagined herself in the train... Day and night, Ilyin is sitting opposite her, never taking his eyes off her, furious at his helplessness and pale with spiritual pain. He calls himself a depraved little schoolboy, abuses her, tears his hair – but once darkness falls, he seizes his moment while the other passengers are falling asleep or getting out to walk along a station platform, and falls on his knees before her, embracing her knees as he did by that bench...

She suddenly realized that she was enjoying this daydream...

"Listen, I won't go on my own!" she said. "You have to come with me!"

"Nonsense, Sofia, that's out of the question!" sighed her husband. "You have to be realistic – there's no sense in wishing for what's impossible."

107

"You'll come with me all right when you find out!" thought Sofia Petrovna.

Once she had decided that whatever happened, she would leave, she felt herself to be out of danger. Gradually her thoughts arranged themselves, her spirits lifted, and she even allowed herself to think about everything. Think what you like, dream what you like, but you're going away, no matter what! Meanwhile her husband was asleep, and gradually the evening drew on… She sat down in the drawing room and played the piano. The lively comings and goings in the street outside, the sound of the music, and above all the thought that she had been so clever and found a solution to her troubles, all thoroughly cheered her up. Other women, her satisfied conscience told her, could never have resisted in her situation, they would have been in an absolute whirl; but she herself had almost burnt up with shame, she had been miserable, and now she was running away from a danger which perhaps was no danger at all! She was so touched by her own virtue and determination that she even took two or three glances at herself in the mirror.

When darkness had fallen, the guests turned up. The men sat down in the dining room to play cards, while the ladies occupied the drawing room and the veranda. Last to arrive was Ilyin. He was gloomy, morose, and looked ill. He sat down at one end of the divan, and never moved from there all evening. Usually lively and talkative, on this occasion he remained silent, scowling and rubbing his eyes. When obliged to answer a question, he forced a smile with his upper lip and gave an abrupt, angry reply. Five times or so he said something witty, but his witticisms came out harsh and cutting. Sofia Petrovna had the impression that he was on the verge of hysteria. Only now, as she sat at the piano, did she see clearly that this miserable man had no stomach for wit, he was sick in his soul, and felt out of place everywhere. For her sake, he was sacrificing the finest days of his youth and his career, wasting the last of his money renting his summer home, abandoning his mother and sisters to their fate; and worst of all – he was wearing himself out in this tormenting inner battle. Common humanity demanded that she should take him seriously...

She could see all this quite clearly, and it pained her very heart; and if at that point she had gone up to Ilyin and simply said "No!", there would have been so much power in her voice that its message would have been hard to miss. But she did not go up to him, did not say that, and did not even think of doing it... The petty selfishness of her youthful nature, so it seemed, had never governed her as strongly as it did that evening. She could feel that Ilyin was miserable, that he was sitting on that divan as though it were a bed of live coals, and she suffered for him; but at the same time, the presence of a man who suffered such agonies of love for her filled her soul with triumph and a sense of her own power. She was aware of her own youth, her beauty, her unattainability, and – since she had resolved to leave! – she allowed herself free rein that evening. She flirted, and giggled without ceasing, and sang with particular feeling and inspiration. Everything delighted her, and she found everything funny. She laughed to herself when she thought back to what had happened by the bench, and the sentry watching them. She found the guests funny, and Ilyin's cutting witticisms, and the pin in his cravat, which she had never noticed before. The pin was in the shape of a little red snake with diamond eyes; she found it so comic, she would have liked to cover it with kisses.

Her singing was tense, with a sort of half-drunk recklessness; and as though wanting to mock another person's grief, she chose sad, melancholy songs about lost hopes, times gone by, old age… "Old age is treading ever closer…" she sang. What did she care about old age?

"I feel there's something bad going on inside me…" she thought from time to time, through her laughter and singing.

The guests dispersed at midnight. The last to leave was Ilyin. Sofia Petrovna still had enough mischief left in her to accompany him as far as the bottom step of the veranda. She felt she wanted to tell him that she was going away with her husband, and to see what effect that had on him.

The moon was hidden behind clouds, but it was light enough for Sofia Petrovna to see the wind playing with the skirts of his overcoat and the awning of the veranda. And she could see how pale Ilyin was, and how he twisted his upper lip as he attempted to smile…

"Sonia, Sonechka… my dearest girl!" he whispered, not allowing her to speak. "My sweet one, my lovely one!"

Overcome with tenderness for her, with a voice filled with tears, he poured out loving words to her, each one more tender than the last, using intimate words to her as if she were his wife or his mistress. He surprised her by passing one arm round her waist, while holding her elbow in the other hand.

"My love, my precious one…" he whispered, kissing her on the nape of her neck. "Be honest, come with me now!"

She slipped out of his embrace and raised her head, all ready to burst out in anger and indignation; but no indignation came out, and all her vaunted virtue and purity barely sufficed for her to come out with the same words that every ordinary woman uses at a time like this:

"You're out of your mind!"

"I mean it, come with me!" Ilyin went on. "Just now, and back there by the bench, Sonia, it was obvious that you're just as helpless as me… You're done for, just as I am! You love me, and now you're wasting time haggling with your conscience…"

Seeing that she was leaving him, he grabbed her by her lace sleeve and hurriedly added:

"If you don't do it today, you will tomorrow – eventually you'll have to give in! Why drag things out? My darling, beloved Sonia, the sentence is passed, so what's the point of putting off its execution? Why try to fool yourself?"

Sofia Petrovna slipped from his grasp and darted in through the door. Back in the drawing room, she closed the piano mechanically, stared for a long time at the music stand, and sat down. She couldn't stand, or even think… After all her reckless excitement, she now felt only fearfully weak, listless and dull. Her conscience whispered that during this past evening she had behaved badly and foolishly, like a wild young girl; that she had just been embracing on the veranda, and even now had an uneasy feeling at her waist and around her elbow. There was not a soul in the drawing room, and only one candle was lit. Lubyantseva sat on the round piano stool, not moving, as if waiting for something to happen. And gradually she succumbed to an overpowering, oppressive desire which seemed to take advantage of her extreme lassitude and of the darkness. It gripped her limbs and her soul like a boa constrictor, growing in strength every second; and now it no longer menaced her as it had done before, but stood openly before her in all its nakedness.

For half an hour she sat there without moving, and making no effort to avoid thinking about Ilyin. Then she rose languidly to her feet and wandered into the bedroom. Andrey Ilyich was already in bed. She sat down by the open window and gave herself over to her desire. She no longer had that "muddle' in her head – all her thoughts and feelings were concentrated on one clear purpose. She tried to fight them, but instantly gave up… Now she understood the enemy's implacable power. Fighting against him would need strength and firmness of purpose, but her birth, upbringing and life had given her no means of support.

"Immoral creature! Disgusting wretch!" she castigated herself for being so helpless. "Is this what you're like?"

Her outraged sense of propriety was so indignant at her helplessness that she called herself all the insulting names she knew, and told herself a great many hurtful and humiliating truths. She told herself, for instance, that she never had been a moral person, and that the only reason she had not succumbed before was that the occasion had never arisen; and that the battle she had been fighting all day had been no more than an amusing farce.

"Perhaps I even did put up a fight," she thought, "but what sort of a fight was it? Even those women who sell themselves put up a fight first; but they still sell themselves. This wasn't much of a fight – just like milk, it only took a day to turn bad! A single day!"

She found herself guilty of the charge that it was neither her emotions, nor Ilyin's personality, that were pulling her away from her home – it was the sensations that awaited her out there… She was nothing but a lady having a fling on her holiday, like so many others!

"That poo-oor little fledgling, his mo-other was killed!" a hoarse tenor voice sang outside the window.

"If I'm going, I'd better go now," thought Sofia Petrovna. Her heart suddenly began pounding terribly hard.

"Andrey!" she almost shrieked. "Listen, we'll... we'll go away, shall we?"

"Yes... I told you before – you go on your own!"

"No, but listen..." she brought out. "If you don't come with me, you might lose me! I think... I've fallen in love!"

"Who with?" asked Andrey Ilyich.

"That shouldn't matter to you, who it is!" cried Sofia Petrovna.

Andrey Ilyich sat up, hung his legs out of the bed, and gazed in astonishment at the dark shape of his wife.

"What a crazy idea!" he yawned.

He didn't believe her, but even so he was frightened. He thought a bit, and asked his wife a number of trivial questions; then he told her what he thought about family life, and infidelity... He talked in an apathetic way for some ten minutes, and got back into bed. His pronouncements were not a success. What a lot of different opinions there are in this world, and a good half of them belong to people who have never suffered misfortune!

Despite the late hour, there were still some summer visitors around. Sofia Petrovna threw on a light cape, and stood and thought for a bit... She still had enough determination left to ask her sleepy husband:

"Are you asleep? I'm going out for a walk... Want to come with me?"

That was her last hope. Receiving no answer, she went out. A cold wind was blowing. Unaware of either the wind or the darkness, she walked on and on… She was being driven by an irresistible force, and if she had stopped, she felt it would have shoved her in the back.

"Immoral creature!" she muttered mechanically. "Disgusting!"

Panting for breath, burning with shame, unaware of her feet carrying her, she was propelled by something more powerful than her shame, her reason, or her fear…

# SERGEANT PRISHIBEYEV

"SERGEANT PRISHIBEYEV! You are hereby charged that on the third day of this month of September you did insult, by words and deeds, Police Constable Zhigin, village elder Alyapov, Police Assistant Yefimov, the witnesses Ivanov and Gavrilov, and a further six villagers, the first three persons named having been subjected to abuse in the course of their official duties. Do you plead guilty to the charge?"

Prishibeyev, a wrinkled, stubble-chinned non-commissioned officer, draws himself up to attention and replies in a hoarse, throaty voice, barking out each word as though shouting a command:

"Your Honour, Mr Justice of the Peace, sir! All the provisions of the law impose a duty to relate every circumstance in reciprocity. It's not me what's guilty but everyone else. This whole business is come about through a dead corpse, God rest its soul. On the third of the month I was proceeding in an orderly manner with my wife Anfisa, when I see a crowd of all different sorts of people standing on the riverbank. By what right have these folk gathered here, I ask myself. What for? Does the law tell people to go swarming about in herds? So I shouted 'Clear off!' And I began pushing people away, ordering them back home, and I told the police assistant to clear them away by the scruff of their necks…"

"Excuse me, but you're not a policeman or an elder – what business is it of yours to chase people away?"

"No business of his! None at all!" The voices rang out from different parts of the courtroom. "He gives us no peace, your Honour! Fifteen years we've been putting up with him! Ever since he came back from the army – it's been enough to drive anyone out of the village. Everyone's sick of him!"

"That's just how it is, your Honour!" said the village elder, a witness in the trial. "The whole community is complaining. There's no living with him! Suppose we're carrying icons in a procession, or there's a wedding, or, you know, something happens – he's always there shouting and kicking up a fuss and ordering people about. He pulls the children by their ears, and spies on the womenfolk in case they're up to anything – just as if he was their father-in-law or something… The other day he was going from house to house telling people not to sing songs or light fires. There's no law, he says, telling people to sing songs."

"Wait a bit, you'll be able to give your evidence later on," says the magistrate. "But now let Prishibeyev go on. Carry on, Prishibeyev!"

"Yessir!" barks the sergeant. "Your Honour, you was good enough to say that it's not my business to disperse people... Very well... But supposing there's some disorder? Is it right to let people cause a disturbance? Where's the law says people have to be let to do as they like? I can't have that, sir. If I don't disperse them, and penalize them, who's going to do it? Nobody don't know how to keep proper order – I'm the only one in the whole village, you might say, your Honour, that knows how to deal with the common people. I understand all about them, your Honour. I'm not a common peasant, I'm a non-commissioned officer, quartermaster-sergeant, retired. I served at Warsaw, at HQ, and after that, for your information, when I was discharged, I was in the fire service, and then on account of my adverse health I left the fire service and served two years as porter in a boys' classical primary school... I know all about regulations, sir. Your peasant, he's a simple fellow, he don't understand a thing, so he has to do as I say, because – it's for his own good. Just look at this here case, for instance. I'm dispersing the crowd, and on the bank there's a drowned cadaver of a deceased person lying on the sand. By what disposition, I ask myself, is he lying there? Is that right and proper? What's the police constable doing, looking on? Why don't you report this to the authorities, constable, I ask him. Maybe this late drowned individual drowned by his own accord, or maybe he didn't and it's something as smells of Siberia. Maybe this here is a case of criminal murder… But Constable Zhigin, he takes no notice, just goes on smoking his fag. Who's this busybody giving orders? he says. Where's he sprung from? As if we didn't know our business without him to tell us, he says. – I can see you don't know it, you idiot, I says, seeing you're just standing there taking no notice. – Reported it to the district police chief yesterday, he says. – Why go to him, I wants to know. What section of the law book says that? That sort of thing, drownings and stranglings and all – the district police chief can't do nothing. This is a criminal matter, I tells him, a civil matter… What you need to do at once, I says, is send a messenger to his Honour the Examining Magistrate and the judges. But the very first thing to do, I tells him, is write an official report and send it to his Honour the Justice of the Peace. But him, that copper, he just stands there listening and laughing at me. And those peasants too. Everybody was laughing, your Honour. I'll swear to that on the Bible. This one here, he was laughing, and him over there, and Zhigin, he was laughing too. What are you all grinning about, I says to them. And the copper says, This sort of thing is nowt to do with the Justice of the Peace. When he said that, I fair lost my rag. Constable, you did say that, didn't you?" he demanded of Constable Zhigin.

"Yes, I did."

"Yes, everybody heard you say those very words, right in front of all the common people. 'This sort of thing is nowt to do with the Justice of the Peace.' Everybody heard you say those… Your Honour, I fair lost my rag, I couldn't believe my ears. Just you say that again, you so-and-so, I tells him, just you repeat those words! And he did, he repeated those very same words. So I went for him. How dare you talk that way about his Honour the Justice of the Peace? A police constable, and you're going against the authorities? Eh? Don't you realize, I tells him, that if his Honour the Justice of the Peace feels like it, he can send you up to gendarmerie headquarters for insubordination? Do you realize, I say, where his Honour could get you packed off to, for all that political talk? Then the elder says, 'The Justice of the Peace,' he says, 'can't issue any orders beyond his own competence. He can only rule on minor matters.' That's what he said – everybody heard him. 'How dare you belittle the authorities?' I tell him. 'I'll not have you playing your games with me, or it'll be the worse for you.' In the old days, when I was at Warsaw or portering at the boys' classical primary school, if ever I heard any unsuitable talk, I'd take a look out onto the street, see if I could see a gendarme. 'Come along this way, soldier,' I'd say, and I'd report the whole thing. But out here in the sticks, who can you report to?… I saw red. I was that upset over people nowadays, forgetting all their duties and turning wilful and disobedient – I took a swing at him and… didn't hit him hard, of course, just a tap, as he deserved, teach him not to use words like that about your Honour… The constable took the elder's side, so I went for him too… That was how it all started… I got worked up, your Honour – well, you've got to sort people out. If you don't beat up a stupid fool, the sin's on your own conscience. Especially when he's deserved it… creating a disturbance…"

"Excuse me! There are people responsible for dealing with disturbances. That's what the constable is for, and the elder, and the police assistant…"

"The constable can't look out for everything. Besides, he don't understand things the way I do."

"But do please realize – this isn't your business!"

"What? What do you mean, not my business? That don't make sense, sir… People behaving disorderly, and it's none of my business? What am I supposed to do, pat them on the back, then? Here they come complaining to you that I won't let 'em sing songs… What's the good of songs, then? Instead of getting on with something sensible, they start singing songs… And then they've all gone for this new fashion, sitting around in the evenings with the fire lit. They ought to be lying down to sleep, not talking and laughing. But I've got 'em all down!"

"Got what down?"

"Them as has their fires lit."

Prishibeyev draws a grubby sheet of paper from his pocket, puts on his glasses and reads:

"Peasants as has fires burning: Ivan Prokhorov, Savva Nikiforov, Piotr Petrov. Soldier's wife Shustrova, widow, lives in flagrant cohabitation with Semion Kislov. Ignat Sverchok does sorcery, and Mavra his wife is a witch, goes out at night and milks other people's cows."

"That'll do!" says the magistrate, and begins questioning the witnesses.

Sergeant Prishibeyev pushes his glasses up on his forehead and stares in amazement at the magistrate, who's evidently not on his side. His bulging eyes gleam, his nose turns crimson. He looks at the magistrate, then at the witnesses, and can't make out why this magistrate is getting so indignant, or why angry murmurs and stifled laughter are breaking out all over the courtroom. Nor can he understand the sentence: one month's detention!

"Whatever for?!" he demands, throwing out his arms in bewilderment. "Where's the law as says that?"

And it's quite clear to him that the world has changed, life has become impossible. He's submerged in dark, gloomy thoughts. But as he walks out of the courtroom and sees the peasants crowding round discussing something, his old habit returns. Unable to control himself, he snaps to attention and shouts in a hoarse, angry voice:

"People – disperse! No crowding! Get along home!"

# THE LADY WITH THE LITTLE DOG

## I

A NEW FACE had appeared on the seafront, they were saying – a lady with a little dog. Dmitry Dmitrich Gurov, who had already spent two weeks at Yalta and knew his way around, had also begun taking an interest in new faces. Sitting in Verney's pavilion, he saw a fair-haired young lady of medium height, wearing a beret, walking past him with a white Pomeranian trotting behind her.

After that he started coming across her several times a day, in the public gardens or the square. She would be walking on her own, always in the same beret, with her white Pomeranian. Nobody knew who she was; she was simply known as "the lady with the little dog".

"If she's here without a husband or friends," thought Gurov, "it wouldn't be a bad idea to get to know her."

He was not yet forty, but he already had a daughter of twelve and two sons at high school. He had been married off young, when only a second-year student, and now he felt that his wife was half as old again as him. She was a tall woman with dark eyebrows who held herself erect and looked stately and dignified; she described herself as a thinking woman. She read a great deal, adopted the modern spelling in her letters, and called her husband not Dmitry but Dimitry, while he secretly regarded her as unintelligent, narrow-minded and dowdy; he was afraid of her, and didn't like being at home. He had begun cheating on her a long time ago, and did it often; that was probably why he almost always expressed a low opinion of women, and when they were talked about in his presence, he would say:

"An inferior race!"

He felt that he had learnt enough, through bitter experience, to be entitled to call them whatever he liked; and yet without that "inferior race" he could not have survived for two days on end. He felt bored and ill at ease in male company, which made him chilly and taciturn; but when he found himself among women, he felt free, he knew what to talk about and how to behave; even saying nothing was easy in their company. His appearance, his character, his whole personality had something intangibly appealing about it that attracted women and made them feel friendly towards him. He knew this, and a force of some kind drew him to them in turn.

Repeated experience, bitter experience indeed, had taught him long ago that for decent people – especially Muscovites, so slow to move and so indecisive – any relationship, while it may initially feel like an agreeable diversion, a charming and light-hearted adventure, invariably develops into a really complicated headache, and the situation eventually becomes intolerable. But at each new encounter with an interesting woman, all his past experience somehow slipped his mind, and he longed to live, and everything seemed so simple and entertaining.

And so it came about one evening that he was dining in the gardens when the lady in the beret approached unhurriedly to sit at the next table. Her expression, her walk, her clothing and coiffure, all told him that she belonged to respectable society, that she was married, visiting Yalta for the first time, on her own, and that she was bored here. There was a great deal of untruth in the stories of immorality in this town, and he despised those stories and knew that they were mostly invented by people who would have been very happy to transgress if only they could; but when the lady sat down at the next table, three paces away from him, he remembered those tales of easy victories, and trips to the mountains, and he was suddenly overcome by the tempting thought of a swift, fleeting love affair, a romance with a strange woman whom he didn't even know by name.

He beckoned coaxingly to the Pomeranian, and when the dog approached he wagged his finger threateningly. The dog growled. Gurov wagged his finger again.

The lady looked at him and at once lowered her eyes.

"He doesn't bite," she said and blushed.

"Can I give him a bone?" And when she nodded, he asked politely, "Have you been in Yalta long?"

"Five days or so."

"I've been stuck here almost two weeks."

Neither spoke for a while.

"Time passes quickly here, but how boring it all is!" she said without looking at him.

"That's what everybody's supposed to say, that it's boring here. Your average man comes from somewhere like Belyov or Zhizdra, and isn't bored there, but when he gets here he goes 'Oh, the tedium! Oh, the dust!' You'd think he came from Granada."

She laughed. Then they carried on eating in silence, like strangers; but after their dinner they walked off side by side – and began a jocular, light-hearted conversation, like free spirits who were pleased with themselves and didn't care where they went or what they talked about. They walked and talked about the strange light on the sea – the water had a soft, warm lilac colour, with a golden streak where the moon was reflected in it. They talked about how sultry it was after the hot day. Gurov said that he came from Moscow, was a philologist by training but worked in a bank; that he had once been trained to sing in a private opera company, but had given it up; that he had two houses in Moscow... And from her he discovered that she had grown up in Petersburg, but had married in S——, where she had now lived for two years; that she was going to spend another month or so in Yalta, and that her husband might come for her then, as he wanted to spend some leave here. She was quite unable to explain where her husband worked – whether it was in the provincial government or the provincial district council – and she herself found that funny. And Gurov also discovered that her name was Anna Sergeyevna.

Later, back in his room, he thought about her and about the fact that she would probably meet him tomorrow. That was bound to happen. As he went to bed, he remembered that she had only very recently been a schoolgirl, and had been studying just as his daughter was doing now; he remembered how diffident and awkward she had been when she laughed, and in conversation with a stranger – this must be the first time in her life that she had found herself alone, in a situation like this, with people following her, and looking at her, and talking to her, all with a single idea in their minds, which she couldn't fail to guess. He remembered her slender, delicate neck, and her pretty grey eyes.

"Still, there's something pathetic about her," he thought as he drifted off to sleep.


II


A week had passed since they had got to know one another. It was a public holiday. Indoors it was stuffy; outdoors the dust was gusting about in eddies and the wind blew people's hats off. Gurov felt thirsty all day, and kept going into the pavilion and offering Anna Sergeyevna a glass of syrup and water or an ice cream. He didn't know what to do with himself.

That evening, when the wind dropped a little, they went out onto the breakwater to watch a steamer coming in. There were a great many people strolling on the quay, waiting to meet people off the boat, and holding bouquets of flowers. Here, he could not fail to notice two striking features of the elegant Yalta crowd: that the elderly ladies dressed like young girls, and there were a great many generals.

Because of the rough sea the boat arrived late, after sunset, and then spent a long time turning around before mooring at the quay. Anna Sergeyevna watched the boat and its passengers through her lorgnette, as if looking for someone she knew, and when she turned to Gurov her eyes were shining. She talked a great deal, asking sudden questions and immediately forgetting what she had asked; then she lost her lorgnette in the crush.

The crowd of well-dressed people was dispersing, it was too dark to see their faces, and the wind had stilled, but Gurov and Anna Sergeyevna went on standing there as if waiting to see whether anybody else would disembark. Anna Sergeyevna stood silently sniffing at her bouquet of flowers, without looking at Gurov.

"The weather's got better this evening," he said. "Where shall we go now? Shall we drive out somewhere?"

She did not answer.

Then he looked hard at her, and suddenly put his arm round her and kissed her on the lips. He was enveloped in the moisture and fragrance of the flowers, and at once looked round anxiously to see if anyone had noticed.

"Let's go to your room..." he said quietly.

And they both walked quickly away.

Her room was stuffy, and smelt of the scent she had bought at a Japanese shop. Looking at her now, Gurov thought "What strange meetings happen in one's life!" Thinking of his past, he remembered carefree, friendly women, who loved light-heartedly and were grateful to him for their happiness, however short-lived; and other women – his wife, for instance – who loved without sincere feeling, with too much talk, and affectation, and hysteria, and with an expression on their faces as if all this wasn't love, or passion, but something more important; and he remembered two or three other women, very beautiful and cold, on whose faces he had suddenly caught a glimpse of a rapacious expression, a determination to seize and take from life more than life could offer – and these were women not in their first youth, who were capricious, unthinking, domineering, unintelligent, and when Gurov cooled towards them, their beauty filled him with hatred, and the lace on their linen reminded him of scales.

But here there was still that diffidence, that angular-
ity of inexperienced youth, a feeling of awkwardness, a
sense of being abashed, as though someone had suddenly
knocked at the door. Anna Sergeyevna, this "lady with
the little dog", was reacting to what had happened in a
peculiar way, very gravely, as if this was her fall: that was
what it seemed like, and it was strange and inappropriate.
Her countenance drooped and seemed faded, and her long
hair hung sadly down at the sides of her face; she was sunk
in reflection, in a dejected posture, like a sinful woman in
an ancient picture.

"This is bad," she said. "You'll be the first to lose your
respect for me now."

On the table in her room lay a watermelon. Gurov cut
himself a slice and began unhurriedly eating it. At least
half an hour went by in silence.

Anna Sergeyevna was a touching figure, redolent of the
purity of a respectable, innocent woman who knew little
of life. The solitary candle burning on the table barely lit
up her face, but it was clear that she was troubled in spirit.

"Why would I lose my respect for you?" asked Gurov.
"You don't know what you're saying."

"God forgive me!" she said, her eyes filling with tears.
"This is dreadful."

"You seem to be justifying yourself."

"How can I justify myself? I'm a low, wicked woman,
I despise myself, I don't even think of justification. It's not

my husband I've deceived, but myself. And not just now – I've been deceiving myself for a long time. My husband may be a good, honest man, but he's a flunkey! I don't know what he does there, what his work is, all I know is that he's a flunkey. I was twenty years old when I married him, I was tormented by curiosity, I wanted something better; life must hold something else, I said to myself. I wanted to live! To live, and live… I was burnt up with curiosity… you won't understand this, but I swear to God, I couldn't control myself, something was happening to me, I couldn't stop myself, and I told my husband I was ill, and came here… And here I kept walking about like a demented person, like a madwoman… and now I've become a vulgar, worthless creature whom everybody has the right to despise."

Gurov was already bored with listening to her, and irritated by her naive language, and all that remorse, so unexpected and out of place. But for the tears in her eyes, he might have thought she was joking or acting a part.

"I don't understand," he said quietly. "What is it you want?"

She buried her head in his chest and pressed herself against him.

"Please, please believe me, I beg you…" she said. "I care about being upright and pure; I find sin revolting, I myself don't know what I'm doing. Simple folk say the Evil One ensnared them. And now I can say that about myself – the Evil One has ensnared me."

"There, there," he muttered.

He looked into her fixed, frightened eyes, and kissed her, and talked gently and quietly to her, and gradually she was comforted, and became cheerful once more, and they both started laughing.

Later, when they went out, there was not a soul on the promenade; the town with its cypresses looked utterly dead, but the sea still murmured as it beat against the shore. A solitary boat was rocking on the waves, with a sleepy light blinking over it.

They found a cab and drove to Oreanda.

"I just found out your surname," said Gurov. "The board down in the hall said Von Diederitz. Is your husband German?"

"No, I believe his grandfather was German, but he's Orthodox himself."

At Oreanda they sat on a bench not far from the church, and looked down in silence at the sea. Yalta could scarcely be seen through the morning mist. White clouds hung motionless over the mountain tops. The leaves on the trees were still, cicadas were chirruping, and the monotonous dull murmur of the sea reaching them from below spoke of repose, of the eternal sleep that awaits us. That same murmur sounded from the sea below before Yalta or Oreanda ever existed; it sounds there now, and will still sound, just as dull and indifferent, when we are no more. And in this constancy, this complete indifference to the life and death of each one of us, there lies hidden, perhaps, a pledge of our everlasting salvation, the ceaseless movement of life on earth, the ceaseless progress towards perfection. As he sat beside this young woman, who looked so beautiful in the dawn light, Gurov felt comforted and enchanted by the sight of his fairy-tale surroundings – the sea, the mountains, the clouds, the expanse of sky – and reflected that in essence, if one really thought about it, everything in this world was beautiful, everything except our own thoughts and actions, when we forget about the higher aims of our existence and our own human dignity.

Someone – no doubt a watchman – came up to them, looked at them and went away. And this little detail also struck him as very mysterious and beautiful. The steamer from Feodosia could be seen arriving, lit up by the sunrise, its lights no longer burning.

"There's dew on the grass," said Anna Sergeyevna after a silence.

"Yes. Time to go home."

They drove back to town.

After that they met on the promenade every day at noon, ate lunch and dinner together, walked about and admired the sea. She complained that she had trouble sleeping, that her heart pounded with anxiety, and kept asking him the same questions over and over again, tormented either by jealousy or by the fear that he didn't respect her enough. And when they were in the square or the gardens, if there was nobody nearby, he would often draw her to him and kiss her passionately. This state of utter idleness, these kisses in broad daylight, looking fearfully over his shoulder in case anybody saw, and the heat, and the smell of the sea, and the constant sight of idle, elegant, well-fed people, seemed to make a new man of him. He would tell Anna Sergeyevna how lovely she was, and how seductive; he was impatiently passionate with her, not moving an inch from her side; while she often became pensive and repeatedly begged him to confess that he didn't respect her, nor love her in the least, but merely saw her as a worthless woman. Almost every day they drove out of town in the late evening, to Oreanda or to the waterfall, and every expedition was a success, always impressing them with the beauty and majesty of the spectacle.

They were expecting her husband to arrive, but a letter came from him to say that he was having trouble with his eyes, and begging his wife to come home at once. Anna Sergeyevna hurriedly prepared to go.

"It's good that I'm leaving," she said to Gurov. "It's fate."

She left by coach, and he went with her. They drove for a whole day. When she got into her compartment on the express train, and the second bell went, she said:

"Come and let me have another look at you. One more look. There."

She was not crying, but she was sad, as though she were unwell, and her face trembled.

"I shall think of you... and remember you," she said. "God bless you, be happy. Don't think ill of me. We're parting for ever, that's how it has to be, because we should never have met. Well, God bless you."

The train moved off quickly, its lights soon vanished, and a minute later no sound of it could be heard, as if everything was conspiring to put an end to this sweet dream, this madness. Left alone on the platform, Gurov gazed into the dim distance and listened to the grasshoppers shrilling and the telegraph wires humming, and felt that he had only just awoken. He reflected that this had been another experience, another adventure in his life, and now it too was over, and what was left to him was the memory of it... He was touched, and sad, and felt a little remorseful; for this young woman whom he would never meet again had not been happy with him. He had been genuinely affectionate towards her, but all the same – the way he treated her, his tone of voice, his caresses, had all carried a slight tinge of mockery, the rough arrogance of a lucky man, and what was more, a man who was almost twice her age. She had always called him kind, exceptional, exalted; she had evidently regarded him as different from what he really was, so he had been unwittingly deceiving her...

There was a smell of autumn here on the station. The evening was chilly.

"High time for me to go north again too," thought Gurov as he left the platform. "High time!"

III

Back in Moscow the winter routine had already started, stoves were lit, and in the mornings when the children drank their tea and got ready for school it was still dark, and their nurses lit the lamps for a while. The frosts had already started. When the first snow falls, on the first day when you ride out on a sleigh, it's good to see the white earth, and white roofs, and draw in soft, wonderful breaths, and remember the days of your youth. The old limes and birches, white with hoarfrost, wear cheerful expressions; they're closer to our hearts than cypresses and palm trees, and when you're near them you no longer want to think of the mountains or the sea.

Gurov was a Muscovite; he had come back to Moscow on a fine, frosty day, and once he had put on his great-coat and warm gloves and gone out for a walk along the Petrovka, and had heard the bells ringing on a Saturday evening, his recent journey and the places he had visited lost all their charm for him. Bit by bit he immersed himself in Moscow life, hungrily read through three newspapers a day, though he claimed never to read the Moscow papers on principle. He was already drawn to restaurants and clubs, dinner parties and celebrations, and felt flattered because he was visited by well-known lawyers and actors, and played cards with a professor at the doctors' club. He could already manage a whole serving of Russian meat stew...

Another month or two would pass, he thought, and Anna Sergeyevna would vanish in the mists of memory, only to reappear once in a while in his dreams, with her touching smile, just as he dreamed of the others. But over a month had passed, it was deepest winter already, and his memory of her was still clear, as though they had only parted yesterday. And his memories glowed ever more vividly. If ever he heard the voices of children preparing their lessons as he sat in his study on a quiet evening, or listened to a song or an organ playing in a restaurant, or if the wind howled in his chimney on a stormy night, his memory at once called everything up – what had happened on the breakwater, and the early morning with the mist on the mountains, and the steamer from Feodosia, and the kisses. He would walk round the room for a long time, remembering, and smiling; and then the memories would turn into dreams, and past events mingled in his mind with what was to come. Anna Sergeyevna was no dream – she followed him around everywhere like a shadow, and haunted him. When he shut his eyes he could see her like a living being, and she seemed more beautiful, younger and more tender than she was; and he seemed to himself to be better than he had been there, in Yalta. In the evenings she gazed at him from the bookshelf, the fireplace, or the corner; he could hear her breathing and the gentle rustle of her dress. In the street he followed women with his eyes, trying to find someone who looked like her…

He was oppressed by a compelling need to share his memories with somebody. But at home he could not talk about his love, and away from home there was no one he could tell. Certainly not his tenants; nor anyone at the bank. And what could he have talked about? Had he really been in love then? Had there really been anything beautiful, poetic, instructive, or even merely interesting, in his relations with Anna Sergeyevna? He found himself reduced to talking vaguely about love, or women, and nobody guessed what it was all about; except that his wife would raise her dark eyebrows and say:

"Dimitry, pretending to be a man about town doesn't suit you a bit."

One night when he left the doctors' club with his partner at cards, he couldn't stop himself exclaiming:

"If only you knew what an enchanting woman I got to know in Yalta!"

The official took his seat on the sledge and drove off, but suddenly turned and called:

"Dmitry Dmitrich!"

"What?"

"You were right just now: that sturgeon was a bit off!"

Those very ordinary words for some reason made Gurov indignant – he felt they were degrading and unclean. What dreadful manners, what people! What pointless nights, and what uninteresting, unremarkable days! All this desperate card-playing, gluttony, drunkenness and endless talk on one single topic. Most of your time and energy goes on pointless activities, and conversations about one and the same thing, and all you're left with at the end is a sort of truncated, wing-clipped life, a rubbishy life; yet you can't run away and escape from it – it's like being shut up in a madhouse or a prison camp!

Gurov lay awake all night, full of indignation, and then had a headache for the whole of the next day. And he slept badly during the following nights, sitting up in bed and thinking, or pacing to and fro in his room. He was fed up with his children, and fed up with the bank, and he didn't feel like going anywhere or talking about anything.

When the December holidays arrived he made preparations to leave, and told his wife he was going to Petersburg to pull strings on some young man's behalf – and he left for S——. What for? He himself didn't really know. He wanted to see Anna Sergeyevna, and talk to her, and arrange a meeting with her if he could.

He arrived at S—— in the morning and took the best room in the hotel. The whole floor was carpeted in grey army cloth, and the table had an inkstand on it, grey with dust, with the figure of a rider on horseback waving his hat in his hand, and with his head broken off. The hotel porter gave him the information he needed: Von Diederitz lived in Old Potters Street, in a house of his own, not far from the hotel. He was rich and lived in style, with his own horses;

everyone in town knew him. The porter pronounced his name "Dridirits".

Gurov took a leisurely stroll to Old Potters Street and found the house. Right opposite the house was a long fence decorated with nails.

"That's a fence one would want to run away from," thought Gurov, looking up at the house windows, and over at the fence, and back again.

He worked out that today was not a working day, so the husband would probably be at home. In any case it would have been tactless to enter the house and cause embarrassment. And if he sent a note, it would probably fall into the husband's hands, and that could spoil everything. The best thing to do was leave it to chance. So he started walking up and down the street and along the fence, waiting for that chance. He saw a beggar go in through the gates, and get attacked by dogs; then, an hour later, he heard a piano being played: the sounds that reached him were faint and indistinct. That must have been Anna Sergeyevna playing. Suddenly the front door opened and an old woman emerged, with the familiar white Pomeranian running after her. Gurov wanted to call the dog, but his heart suddenly started pounding, and in his anxiety he couldn't remember the dog's name.

He went on walking up and down, loathing the grey fence more and more, and had already decided in his annoyance that Anna Sergeyevna had forgotten about him, and indeed might be amusing herself with some other man. That would have been quite natural in this young woman's situation, forced to look out at that damned fence from morning to night. He went back to his hotel room and spent a long time sitting on his sofa, not knowing what to do; then he had dinner, and took a long nap.

"How stupid and upsetting all this is," he thought when he woke up and looked at the dark windows. It was late evening. "I've slept all I want, for some reason. What am I going to do all night now?"

He was sitting on his bed, covered with a cheap grey blanket that might have come from a hospital. In his irritation, he tormented himself with the thought:

"So much for your Lady with the Little Dog... So much for your adventure... Now you can just sit here."

That same morning at the station, he had noticed a poster in huge print: the premiere of *The Geisha* was on that evening. Now he remembered that, and drove to the theatre.

"It's quite possible that she goes to premieres," he thought.

The theatre was full. As in every provincial theatre, there was a fog above the candelabra, the gallery was full of noise and excitement; the local dandies were standing in the front row, hands behind their backs, waiting for the performance to begin; and here, in the front seat of the Governor's box, was the Governor's daughter in a feather boa, while the Governor himself hid modestly behind the door and only his hands could be seen. The curtain swayed, the orchestra spent ages tuning up. Spectators were coming in and taking their seats; and all this time Gurov was eagerly searching with his eyes.

And Anna Sergeyevna entered. She sat down in the third row, and when Gurov looked at her, he felt a tightening of the heart and understood clearly that there was nobody closer or dearer or more important to him in the whole world now than her. Lost as she was in this provincial crowd, this small and in no way remarkable woman, holding a vulgar lorgnette in her hand, now filled his whole life. She was his grief and his joy, the only happiness that he wished for now. And listening to the sounds of the second-rate orchestra, the wretched provincial fiddles, he thought about how beautiful she was. He thought, and he dreamed.

When she entered the theatre, Anna Sergeyevna was accompanied by a young man with short side whiskers, who sat down beside her. He was very tall, and walked with a stoop; at every step he nodded his head, and seemed to be constantly greeting people. This was probably her husband, whom in Yalta she had once described, in an outburst of bitterness, as a flunkey. And indeed, with his lanky figure, and his side whiskers, and his little bald patch, there was something of the obsequious flunkey about him. He had a simpering smile, and there was some sort of badge of office in his buttonhole, like a footman's number.

During the first interval the husband went out for a smoke, while she remained in her seat. Gurov, who also had a seat in the stalls, went over to her and said in a trembling voice, with a forced smile:

"Good evening."

She looked up at him and turned pale; then she looked again, horrified and unable to believe her eyes. She clenched her fingers round her fan and lorgnette together, evidently struggling to keep herself from fainting. Neither spoke. She sat, he stood before her, alarmed by her confusion and not daring to sit down beside her. The violins and the flute sang out as they were tuned, and they had the frightening feeling that the spectators in all the boxes were looking at them. But then she stood up and walked quickly to the exit; he followed her; and they both walked without knowing where they were going, along corridors, up and down stairs, catching glimpses of people wearing the uniforms of judges, teachers, civil servants, all with their badges; there were ladies, and fur coats hanging up, and a draught that filled the place with the smell of cigarette ends. And Gurov, his heart pounding, thought:

"O God! What's the point of all these people, and this orchestra?…"

And at that moment he suddenly remembered standing at the station that other evening, seeing Anna Sergeyevna off and telling himself that it was all over, that they'd never meet again. How far that had been from the end of it all!

She stopped on a dark, narrow staircase, under a sign saying "To the Amphitheatre".

"How you frightened me!" she said, breathing in gasps, still pale and quite overcome. "Oh, how you frightened me! I almost died. Why are you here? What have you come for?"

"Please understand, Anna, you have to understand…" he said hastily under his breath. "I beg you, you must see…"

She looked at him with eyes full of terror, and entreaty, and love; she stared at him, trying to fix his features for ever in her memory.

"I'm suffering so much!" she went on, not listening to him. "All this time I've only ever thought about you, I've lived by thinking about you. And I wanted to forget – to forget – but why, why have you come here?"

There were two high school boys on the landing above, smoking and looking down at them, but Gurov didn't care, he drew Anna Sergeyevna to him and began kissing her face, her cheeks, her arms…

"What are you doing? What are you doing?" she said in alarm, trying to push him away. "We've gone mad, you and I. You must leave today, straight away… I beg you by all that's holy, I implore you… Someone's coming!"

Someone was climbing the stairs from below.

"You have to leave…" Anna Sergeyevna went on in a whisper. "Do you hear, Dmitry Dmitrich? I'll come to Moscow to see you. I've never been happy, and now I'm miserable, and I'll never, ever be happy, never! Don't make me suffer even more! I promise faithfully, I'll come to Moscow. But now we have to separate! My sweet, kind, dear one, we must part!"

She squeezed his hand and quickly set off down the stairs, repeatedly looking round at him, and her eyes showed how unhappy she really was. Gurov stayed where he was for a while, listening, and when all the sounds had died away he hunted out his overcoat on its hanger and left the theatre.

IV

And Anna Sergeyevna began coming to visit him in Moscow. Once every two or three months she would leave S—— and tell her husband she was going to consult a professor about her woman's disorder – and her husband believed her and didn't believe her. When she arrived in Moscow, she would stay at the Slavonic Bazaar hotel and at once send Gurov a messenger in a red cap. Gurov visited her there, and nobody in Moscow knew.

One day he was on his way to her like this on a winter morning. The messenger had been at his house the previous evening and not found him at home. Now he was walking with his daughter, because he wanted to see her to school and it was on his way. Heavy wet snowflakes were falling.

"It's three degrees above zero, and yet it's snowing," said Gurov to his daughter. "But of course it's only warm here on the earth's surface – the temperature in the upper atmosphere is quite different."

"Papa, why aren't there thunderstorms in winter?"

He explained that too. He talked, while thinking about the fact that here he was, on his way to an assignation, and not a living soul knew, and probably never would. He had two lives: an open one which everyone saw and knew about if they cared to, full of conventional truths and conventional deceits, just like the lives of all his friends and acquaintances; and another life that ran its course in secret. And through some strange chain of circumstances, perhaps just a chance one, everything that was important or interesting or essential for him, everything in which he was honest and did not deceive himself, everything that constituted the core of his life, happened in secret from everyone else; while everything that made up his lies, the cloak he hid behind to conceal the truth – his work at the bank, for instance, and his arguments at the club, and his talk about "the inferior race", and attending celebratory dinners with his wife – all that was out in the open. And he judged everyone else like himself, not believing what he could see and always assuming that each person led his own real, interesting life in secret, under cover of night as it were. Each individual existence relies on secrecy; that may be part of the reason why a civilized person is so anxious to ensure that privacy is respected.

He left his daughter at her school and set off for the Slavonic Bazaar. He took off his greatcoat downstairs, went up and knocked quietly at a door. Anna Sergeyevna, wearing the grey dress he loved so much, was worn out by her journey and her wait; she had been expecting him ever since the evening before. She was pale, looked at him without smiling, and as soon as he entered the room she fell on his chest. Their kiss was a long, protracted one, as if they hadn't seen each other for two years or more.

"Well, how's life?" he asked. "What's new?"

"Wait... I'll tell you in a minute... I can't."

She could not talk because she was weeping. Turning away from him, she pressed her handkerchief to her eyes.

"Well, let her cry a bit; I'll wait," he thought, and sat down in an armchair.

Then he rang for some tea; and later, when he was drinking his tea, she was still standing by the window with her back to him. She was weeping with agitation, with the bitter realization that their lives had turned out so tragically: only seeing each other in secret, hiding from other people like thieves! Hadn't their lives been ruined?

"Come on, do stop!" he said.

It was obvious to him that this love of theirs was not going to end soon – who knew when? Anna Sergeyevna was becoming ever more attached to him, she adored him, and it would be unthinkable to tell her that all this would end one day. Nor would she have believed it.

He went up to her and put his hands on her shoulders to caress her, and make light of things, and at that moment he saw himself in the mirror.

His hair was already turning grey. He found it strange that he had aged so much in recent years, and lost his looks. The shoulders on which his hands rested were warm and quivering. He felt compassion for this life, still so warm and beautiful, but probably close to the time when it would start to fade and wilt like his own. Why did she love him so much? He always appeared to women not as what he really was, and what they loved in him was not himself but the man created by their imagination, the man they had been desperately seeking all their life. And then when they realized their mistake, they went on loving him just the same. But not one of them had been happy with him. Time passed, he met a person, they became close, and then parted; but he had never been in love. There had been anything you like, but not love.

And only now, when his hair had turned grey, had he fallen in love, properly, genuinely – for the first time in his life.

He and Anna Sergeyevna loved each other like people very close and dear to one another, like husband and wife, like dearest friends; they felt that fate itself had marked them out for each other, and it was impossible to understand why he had a wife and she a husband. It was as if they were a pair of birds of passage, male and female, who had been caught and forced to live in separate cages. They had forgiven each other for what they were ashamed of in their own past, they forgave everything in the present, and felt that this love of theirs had brought about a change in each of them.

In the past, in moments of sadness, he had consoled himself with all kinds of arguments, anything that came into his head; but now he had no use for arguments, he felt profound compassion, and wanted to be sincere and tender...

"That's enough, my darling," he said. "You've had a cry, and that'll do... Now let's talk – we'll think of something."

Then they had a long discussion, talking about how to escape from the need for concealment, and deceit, and living in different towns, and not seeing one another for long periods. How could they break free from this unbearable bondage?

"But how? How?" he asked, holding his head in his hands. "How?"

And they felt that before long there would be a solution, and then they would enter on a new and wonderful life. But they could both see clearly that the end was a long, long way off, and the most difficult and complicated part was only just beginning.

# THE HUNTSMAN

A STIFLING, SULTRY NOONDAY. Not a wisp of cloud in the sky… The sun-scorched grass has a sad, hopeless look: though rain will come, this grass will never be green again… The forest stands still and silent, as if the treetops were staring out at something, or waiting in expectation.

Along the edge of the clearing comes a tall, narrow-shouldered man of forty-odd years, in a red shirt, patched trousers from some gentleman's wardrobe and high boots, trudging along the path with a lazy, shambling, slouching gait. To his right is a green glade; to his left, a golden sea of ripe rye stretches to the far horizon. He is red-faced and sweating. On his handsome blond head he wears a jaunty-looking white cap with a straight peak like a jockey's: evidently a gift from an open-handed young gentleman. Over his shoulder hangs his game bag, with a mangled blackcock in it. He is carrying a double-barrelled shotgun, both triggers cocked, and squinting at his scrawny old dog as it runs ahead of him sniffing at the bushes. All around is quiet, not a sound is heard… Everything living has taken shelter from the heat.

"Yegor Vlasych!" The hunter suddenly hears a quiet voice.

He starts, looks round, and frowns. Beside him, as though she had risen up through the ground, stands a pale peasant woman of thirty or so, carrying a sickle. She tries to look into his face, and gives a shy smile.

"Oh, it's you, Pelageya!" says the huntsman, stopping and slowly uncocking the gun. "Hmm!... How did you get here?"

"Women from our village are working here, so I came with them... I'm a labourer, Yegor Vlasych."

"Uh-huh..." mumbles Yegor Vlasych, and he walks slowly on.

Pelageya follows him. They walk twenty steps or so in silence.

"It's a long time since I saw you last, Yegor Vlasych..." says Pelageya, gazing tenderly at the huntsman's shoulders as he moves. "Ever since Holy Week, when you looked into our hut for a minute and had a drink of water – we haven't seen you since then... Dropped in for a minute in Holy Week, and God knows what a state you were in then... drunk and all... swore at me, beat me up, and walked out... and I've been waiting, and waiting... worn my eyes out with watching for you... Oh, Yegor Vlasych, Yegor Vlasych! If only you'd come by sometime!"

"What am I supposed to do at your place?"

"Well, there's nothing for you to do, of course, but still... there's the household... you could look and see how things are going... You're the master... Look at that, you've shot a blackcock, Yegor Vlasych! Look, why don't you sit down, have a rest?"

All this time as she is talking, Pelageya giggles like a silly girl, and gazes up into Yegor's face... Her own face is just radiant with joy...

"Sit down? Why not..." says Yegor indifferently, and picks a spot between two fir trees growing side by side. "What are you standing for? Sit down yourself!"

Pelageya sits down a little way off, in the full glare of the sunlight. She's ashamed of her happiness, and hides her smile behind her hand. A couple of minutes pass in silence.

"You might drop in just once," says Pelageya softly.

"What for?" sighs Yegor, taking off his little cap and wiping his flushed forehead with a sleeve. "There's no point. If I drop in for a couple of hours, it just creates a fuss and gets you all worked up; and living in the village the whole time – I couldn't stand that... You know yourself, I'm spoilt... I need a proper bed, and decent tea, and refined conversation... and for everything to be nice around me; but back in your village there's nothing but poverty and squalor... I wouldn't last a day there. If there was a decree, say, ordering me to live with you, then I'd either set fire to the hut, or do away with myself. I've been pampered like that ever since I was a child – I can't help it."

"So where are you living now?"

"At Dmitry Ivanich the landowner's place – I'm his huntsman. I supply him with game for his table, but actually… he keeps me because he likes to have me there."

"That's not a proper job, Yegor Vlasych… Other people do it for fun, but for you it's like your trade… your real occupation."

"You don't understand, stupid," says Yegor, gazing thoughtfully up at the sky. "You've never in your life understood me, and you never will understand the kind of man I am… You think I'm no good, I've lost my way in life; but anybody with a bit of understanding can see that I'm the best shot in the whole district. The gentry can see that – I've even been written about in the paper. There's not one man my equal as a sportsman… And if I despise your rustic life, that doesn't mean I'm too proud or too pampered. Ever since I was a little boy, you see, I've never known any occupation outside my gun and my dogs. If they took my gun away I'd get out my fishing line; if they took that away I'd get by with my bare hands. Horses, too – I've made money that way, scouting round markets when I had the cash. And you know yourself that when a peasant goes to work as a huntsman or a horse dealer, that's goodbye to his plough. If a man gets a taste for freedom, you'll never root it out of him. Just like your gentleman: if he goes off to be an actor or some other sort of artist, he'll never make an official or a landowner. You're a woman, you don't understand – but you need to understand."

"I do understand, Yegor Vlasych."

"Well, you obviously don't understand, if you're starting to cry."

"I'm… I'm not crying…" says Pelageya, looking away. "It's a sin, Yegor Vlasych! You might come and live with me, just for one day – I'm so unhappy. It's been twelve years since I married you, and… we've never once made love! I'm not… not crying…"

"Love…" mutters Yegor, scratching his arm. "There can't be any love. It's nothing but words, you and me being husband and wife – is that what we really are? For you I'm a wild man, and for me you're nothing but a simple peasant woman who doesn't understand a thing. What kind of a match are we for one another? I'm a free spirit, pampered, loose-living, and you're a working woman, you go around in bark shoes, you live in the dirt and never straighten your back. I see myself as a first-rate hunter, but you look at me and feel sorry for me. What kind of a couple do we make?"

"But we're married, Yegor Vlasych!" sobs Pelageya.

"Not married of our own free will… Have you forgotten? You can thank Count Sergey Pavlich… and yourself. The Count was so jealous because I was a better shot than him, he filled me up with vodka for a month on end. When a person's that drunk, you could make a heathen of him, never mind marrying him off. He took me when I was drunk and married me off to you for revenge… Married a huntsman to a cowherd girl! You could see

I was drunk – why did you take me? You weren't a serf, you could have said no! Of course it's a piece of luck for a cowherd girl to marry a huntsman, but you ought to have thought it through. So now you have to suffer and cry. The Count's had his laugh, and you're left to cry… and bang your head against the wall…"

There is a silence. Three wild ducks fly over the clearing. Yegor looks up at them and follows them with his eyes until they are no more than three barely visible dots, flying down to land somewhere far beyond the forest.

"What do you live on?" he asks, turning from the ducks to look at Pelageya.

"At the moment I'm going out to work, and in the winter I take in a baby from the orphanage and bottle-feed it. They pay me a rouble and a half a month."

"Uh-huh…"

Another silence. A quiet song rises up from the harvested strip of the rye field, but breaks off as soon as it has started. It's too hot to sing…

"They say you've built Akulina a new hut," says Pelageya.

Yegor says nothing.

"So you must fancy her…"

"That's how your life's turned out, can't be helped!" says the hunter, stretching himself. "You have to put up with it, poor thing. Anyway, I must go, I've been talking too long… I have to get to Boltovo by evening…"

Yegor stands up, stretches and slings the gun over his shoulder. Pelageya gets up too.

"So when are you coming to the village?" she asks softly.

"No point. I'll never come when I'm sober, and I'm not much use to you drunk. I get nasty then… Goodbye."

"Goodbye, Yegor Vlasych…"

Yegor perches his cap on the back of his head, clicks his tongue at the dog, and walks off. Pelageya stands still and watches him go… She sees his shoulders swinging, his rakish head, his careless, lazy gait, and her eyes fill with sadness and loving tenderness… She rests her glance on her husband's tall, slender form, caressing him, fondling him… As if he can feel that look, he stops and turns his head… He says nothing, but his face and his raised shoulders tell Pelageya that he wants to say something. Timidly she walks up to him and gazes at him with imploring eyes.

"Here!" he says, looking away.

He hands her a tattered rouble note, and quickly walks off.

"Goodbye, Yegor Vlasych…" she says, mechanically taking the rouble.

He follows the long pathway, straight as a taut strap… Pale and motionless as a statue, she stands there, hungrily watching every step he takes. But now the red of his shirt merges with the dark colour of his trousers, she can't make out his footsteps, she can't distinguish his dog from his

ANTON CHEKHOV

boots. All she can see is his little cap – but suddenly Yegor turns sharply into a clearing on the right, and the little cap vanishes into the greenery.

"Goodbye, Yegor Vlasych…" whispers Pelageya, standing on tiptoe to catch a last glimpse of his little white cap.

# THE PRIVY COUNCILLOR

I N EARLY APRIL 1870 my mother Klavdia Arkhipovna, a lieutenant's widow, received a letter from Petersburg from her brother Ivan, who was a privy councillor. Among other things, this letter said: "My liver disease obliges me to live abroad every summer; but as I have no spare money at present for a journey to Marienbad, it's quite possible, dear sister, that I shall spend this summer with you at your house at Kochuyevka…"

On reading this letter, my mother grew pale and trembled all over; then her face took on an expression of mingled joy and sadness. She started crying and laughing. This battle between tears and laughter always reminds me of a hot candle flickering and crackling when water is splashed on it. Mother read the letter through once more, then summoned the whole household and explained to us all, in a voice shaking with agitation, that there had been four Gundasov brothers in all: one of the Gundasovs had died in infancy, a second entered the army and also died, the third – not wishing to speak ill of him – was an actor, while the fourth…

"The fourth has left us all far behind," sobbed Mother. "He's my own brother, we grew up together, but now I'm all of a tremble… A privy councillor, he is, a general! How am I going to welcome him, my angel brother? What shall I talk to him about, ignorant fool that I am? Fifteen years I haven't seen him! Andryushenka," Mother said to me, "be happy, you little silly! What a stroke of luck for you that God is sending him to us!"

After we had heard every detail of the history of the Gundasovs, the whole estate was plunged into such turmoil as I'd only been used to seeing in the days coming up to Christmas. Nothing was spared but the sky above and the water in the river; everything else was cleaned, washed down and repainted. If the sky had been lower and smaller, and the river hadn't flowed so fast, they too would have been scoured with brick dust and scrubbed with a cloth. Our walls were white as snow, but they were whitewashed anew; the floors were bright and shining, but they were washed every day. Our cat Bobtail (as a child I had cut off a good quarter of his tail with the knife meant for splitting the sugarloaf, hence his nickname of Bobtail) was carried out of our rooms to the kitchen and handed over to Anisya's care; and Fedka was warned that if the dogs came anywhere near the porch, then "God would punish him". But nobody was punished as hard as the poor divans, armchairs and carpets! Never before had they been thrashed so soundly with sticks as now, in readiness for our guest. My pigeons took fright at the thumping of the sticks, and kept flying up into the sky.

Spiridon the tailor at Novostroyevka, the only tailor in the whole district brave enough to sew for the gentry, used to come over to us; he was a teetotaller, hard-working, good at his job, and not without some imagination and a feeling for form; but for all that, his tailoring was appalling. It was his anxiety that spoiled everything... The fear that his work wasn't sufficiently modish made him alter everything five times over, going off to town on foot just to study the dandies, and finally dressing us in outfits that even a cartoonist would have considered overdone caricatures. We paraded around in impossibly tight trousers, and jackets so short that we always felt embarrassed when young ladies were present.

This Spiridon spent ages taking my measurements. He measured all of me, up, down and sideways, as if preparing to fit barrel hoops around me, then he took ages making notes in thick pencil on a piece of paper, and marked up all his measurements with triangular signs. When he had finished with me, he went on to my tutor Yegor Alexeyevich Pobedimsky. This unforgettable tutor of mine was just then passing through the stage where men check how their moustaches are growing, and adopt a critical attitude towards clothing, so you can imagine the holy terror that gripped Spiridon when he took on my tutor! Yegor Alexeyevich was made to throw back his head, part his legs in an inverted Y, and alternately raise and lower his arms. Spiridon measured him several times over, stepping round him like a lovelorn pigeon around his mate, getting down on one knee, bending over double… My exhausted mother, worn out by all the fuss and red in the face from the hot flat irons, gazed at all this long rigmarole and said:

"You watch out, Spiridon, God will punish you if you spoil the cloth. You'll never know happiness again if you don't get this right!"

Mother's words threw Spiridon into fevers and sweats, because he was sure he wouldn't get it right. He charged one rouble twenty kopeks for making my suit, and two roubles for Pobedimsky's, while we supplied the cloth, linings and buttons. That wasn't really expensive, especially as Novostroyevka was some seven miles from us, and the tailor came four times for fittings. At those fittings, when we squeezed ourselves into the narrow trousers and jackets all covered with basting threads, Mother would always frown disapprovingly and say in astonishment:

"God knows what the fashions are coming to nowadays! I'm ashamed even to look at this. If my brother didn't live in the capital, I'd never dream of getting you fashionable clothes!"

Spiridon was pleased that fashion was getting the blame rather than himself, and shrugged his shoulders as if to say "Nothing to be done – that's the spirit of the time!"

The excitement with which we awaited our guest's arrival can only be compared to the feeling of suspense at a spiritualist séance, as the medium awaits the imminent appearance of a spirit. Mother suffered migraines and kept bursting into tears. I lost my appetite, slept badly and neglected my lessons. Even in my dreams, I was constantly longing to see a general as soon as I could – that is, a man wearing epaulettes, an embroidered collar riding up as high as his ears, and carrying a drawn sabre in his hand – just like the man in the picture over the divan in our drawing room, who glared with his terrifying dark eyes at anyone bold enough to look at him. Only Pobedimsky still felt at ease. He was neither terrified nor delighted; but occasionally, when he listened to my mother telling the story of the Gundasov family, he would say:

"Yes, it'll be nice to have someone fresh to talk to."

My tutor was regarded by the people on our estate as someone quite out of the ordinary. He was a young man of twenty or so with a pimply complexion, shaggy hair, a low brow and an unusually long nose – so long that when he wanted to take a close look at something, he was obliged to cock his head to one side like a bird. As far as we were concerned, there was no one as clever, as well-educated or as stylish as him in the whole province. He had completed all six classes of high school, and then enrolled at the veterinary school, from which he was expelled before he had been there six months. He kept the reason for his expulsion very dark, which allowed anyone that way inclined to see him as a man who had suffered, and to some extent as a man of mystery. He spoke little, and only about learned subjects, ate meat during the fasts, and always viewed life around him with haughty disdain – though that never stopped him accepting presents such as suits of clothes from my mother, or decorating my kites with silly faces and red teeth. Mother disliked him for his "pride", but was in awe of his intellect.

Our guest did not keep us waiting long. In early May, two wagonloads of big trunks arrived from the station. The trunks looked so majestic that the drivers, as they unloaded them, instinctively doffed their caps.

"I suppose those trunks must be full of uniforms and gunpowder…" I thought to myself.

Why gunpowder? Probably the notion of a general was closely bound up in my mind with cannon and gunpowder.

When I awoke on the morning of 10th May, my nurse whispered to me that "His Excellency your uncle" had arrived. I dressed quickly, washed after a fashion, skipped my prayers and rushed downstairs. In the hallway I bumped into a tall, corpulent gentleman with modish side whiskers and a dandified overcoat. Overcome with holy terror, I approached him and, remembering the ceremonial drawn up by my mother, scraped back one foot, bowed low and made to kiss his hand; but the gentleman withdrew his hand and explained that he was not my uncle but merely Piotr, my uncle's valet. The sight of this Piotr, dressed far more splendidly than Pobedimsky or me, filled me with profound astonishment, which to tell the truth has remained with me to this day. Is it possible that such solid, dignified men, with intelligent, stern faces, can just be lackeys? What does it all mean?

Piotr told me that my mother and uncle were in the garden. I rushed out to find them.

Nature, knowing nothing of the history of the Gundasovs or of my uncle's rank, was feeling far more free and relaxed than I was. The garden was a scene of such commotion as one only ever sees at a fair. Countless starlings skimmed through the air and hopped around the paths, noisily twittering as they hunted for May beetles. Flocks of sparrows filled the lilac bushes, which thrust their tender fragrant blossoms straight into your face. At every turn, the air was full of the song of golden orioles and the shrill cries of hoopoes and red-footed falcons. At any other time I would have been hunting for dragonflies or chucking stones at the raven perched on a little hummock under an aspen tree, turning his blunt beak this way and that. But now I was in no mood for mischief – my heart was pounding, I felt cold in the pit of my stomach; I was preparing to meet a man with epaulettes, a drawn sabre, and terrifying eyes!

Imagine my disappointment! Strolling about the garden by Mother's side was a skinny little dandy wearing white silk trousers and a white cap. He had his hands in his pockets, his head thrown back, and he kept running ahead of Mother; he seemed to be quite a young man. There was so much movement and life in his whole body that I could see no signs of treacherous old age in him until I approached him from behind and looked up at the headband of his cap, beneath which some close-cropped silver hairs could be seen. Instead of the solid, stiff movements of a general, I saw an almost schoolboyish fidgetiness; instead of a stiff collar pushing up at his ears, an ordinary pale-blue neckcloth. Mother and uncle were strolling along a path and chatting. I came quietly up behind them and waited for one of them to look round.

"What a delightful place you have here, Klavdia!" said my uncle. "How sweet and charming it is! If I'd known you had such a lovely home, nothing would have induced me to spend all those years going abroad."

My uncle quickly bent forward and sniffed at a tulip. Everything he saw delighted him and roused his curiosity, as if he had never before in his life seen a garden or a sunny day. This strange man seemed to bounce around on springs, and never stopped chattering, never allowing my mother to get a word in. All of a sudden Pobedimsky appeared from behind an elder tree at a bend in the path. This was so unexpected that my uncle gave a start and took a step backwards. On this occasion my tutor was wearing his best long-sleeved cape, which (particularly from behind) made him look very like a windmill. He had a solemn and majestic air. Pressing his hat to his breast in the Spanish style, he took a step towards my uncle and bowed the way marquesses bow in melodramas – forwards and a little sideways.

"I have the honour to present myself to your Excellency," he announced in a loud voice. "Tutor and instructor to your nephew, formerly enrolled at the Veterinary Institute, nobleman Pobedimsky!"

Such courtesy on the part of my tutor greatly pleased Mother. She smiled, and froze in the pleasant expectation that he would make some other clever remark; but my tutor, expecting that his majestic greeting would bring a majestic response, in other words that he would receive a lordly "Hm!" from the general and be offered a pair of fingers to shake, was deeply embarrassed and cowed to receive from my uncle a friendly laugh and a firm handshake. He muttered a few more incoherent words, coughed and stood aside.

"Well, isn't that nice now?" laughed my uncle. "Just look: he puts on a cloak and thinks he's ever so clever! I like that, upon my soul!… What youthful aplomb, what life, in that silly cloak! And who's this lad?" he asked, turning and suddenly catching sight of me.

"This is my Andryushenka," said my mother, presenting me with a blush. "My pride and joy…"

I scraped my foot over the sand and performed a deep bow.

"A fine lad… fine lad…" muttered my uncle, withdrawing his hand which I was attempting to kiss, and stroking my head. "So you're called Andryusha, eh? Fine, fine… Mm-yes… upon my soul… At school, are you?"

Mother began to describe my brilliance at school and my excellent behaviour, fibbing and exaggerating as all mothers do, while I walked beside my uncle and, in accordance with prescribed ceremonial, never stopped making low bows. When Mother started dropping hints about what a good idea it would be for a boy with my remarkable talents to get into the cadet corps on a government grant, and when I, in accordance with prescribed ceremonial, was supposed to burst into tears and beg my uncle for his patronage, my uncle stopped dead and flung out his arms in astonishment.

"Goodness gracious! What have we here?" he demanded.

Advancing straight towards us along the path came Tatyana Ivanovna, the wife of our bailiff Fyodor Petrovich. She was carrying a starched white petticoat and a long ironing board. As she passed us she glanced timidly through lowered eyelashes at our guest, and blushed crimson.

"Just one thing after another…" muttered my uncle through his teeth, tenderly watching her retreating figure. "At your home, my sister, every step brings a new surprise…"

"She's our beauty," said Mother. "We sent for her all the way from town, seventy miles off, to be Fyodor's bride."

Not everyone would have called Tatyana Ivanovna a beauty. She was a plump little thing of twenty or so, quite graceful, with an attractive rosy face and dark eyebrows, but her face and her whole person were devoid of any striking feature; there was not a single bold line to catch the eye, as if nature in creating her had run out of inspiration and resolve. Tatyana Ivanovna was timid, shy and well-mannered, walked smoothly and quietly, spoke little, rarely laughed, and her whole life was as even and flat as her face and her smooth, slicked-down hair. My uncle screwed up his eyes and smiled as he gazed after her. Mother looked sharply at his smiling face and turned serious.

"And so you never married, brother!" she sighed.

"No, I never married."

"Why was that?" Mother asked gently.

"What can I say? That's how my life turned out. When I was young I was too hard-working, I had no time for living, and later when I wanted to live – I looked around and saw fifty years behind my back. I was too late! But… it's depressing, talking about all that."

My mother and uncle both sighed in unison and walked on, while I dropped back and ran off to find my tutor and share my impressions with him. Pobedimsky was standing in the middle of the courtyard, solemnly gazing up at the sky.

"He's obviously a cultured man," he said, twisting his head to look at me. "I hope we get on."

An hour later Mother came to find us.

"My darlings, I have a terrible problem!" she panted. "My brother has arrived with his valet, and that valet, God help him, isn't the sort of person you could put up in the kitchen or the hallway – he's absolutely got to have a room of his own. I can't think what to do with him! Unless – couldn't you, my children, perhaps move into Fyodor's hut for a time? And then we'd give the valet your room, eh?"

We willingly agreed, because we'd have far more freedom living in the hut than under Mother's eye in the house.

"It's an absolute disaster!" Mother went on. "My brother says he won't dine at midday but after six in the evening, the way they do in Petersburg. I'm simply at my wits' end! By seven at night the whole dinner will be spoilt in the oven. Honestly, men don't understand the first thing about running a household, for all they're so clever. There's no help for it, we'll have to cook two dinners! You, my children, can carry on eating your dinner at midday, but your poor old mother will have to hold out till seven for my dear brother's sake."

Mother heaved a deep sigh, told me to try and please my uncle whom God had sent as a stroke of luck for me, and ran off to the kitchen. That same day Pobedimsky and I moved over to the hut. We were put up in a through room between the hallway and the bailiff's bedroom.

Despite my uncle's arrival and our move, our lives unexpectedly carried on much as before – dull and monotonous. We were excused lessons "on account of the guest". Pobedimsky, who never read or occupied himself in any way, generally sat on his bed tracing patterns in the air with his long nose, thinking about something or other. From time to time he would get up, try on his new suit, and then sit down again to think in silence. Only one thing bothered him – the flies, which he mercilessly slapped with the palms of his hands. After dinner he would generally "have a rest", and his snores upset everyone on the estate. I would be running about the gardens from morning till night, or sitting in the hut building kites. During the first two or three weeks we didn't see much of my uncle. He would spend whole days on end sitting and working in his room, despite the flies and the heat. His extraordinary capacity for sitting glued to his table seemed to us a sort of inexplicable conjuring trick. We idle folk knew nothing of regular work, and his assiduity struck us as nothing short of a miracle. He woke at nine every day, sat down at his table and never rose from it till dinnertime; after dinner he would go back to his work, and carry on with it till late at night. When I peeped through his keyhole, I only ever saw one and the same thing: my uncle sitting at his table, working. The work consisted in writing with one hand while the other leafed through a book; and very oddly, his whole body was in constant move-ment, his leg swinging like a pendulum, while he whistled a tune and nodded his head in time with it. He wore a very absent-minded and light-hearted expression, as if he wasn't working but playing noughts and crosses. I always saw him wearing his short, dandified jacket and a jauntily tied cravat, and he always smelt – even through the keyhole – of some delicate feminine perfume. The only thing that brought him out of his room was his dinner; but he didn't eat much.

"I can't understand my brother!" Mother complained. "Every day we kill a turkey and some pigeons just for him, and I make him a fruit compote with my own hands, and then he just swallows a bowl of soup and eats a little finger of meat, and leaves the table. And if I beg him to eat some more, he sits down again and drinks some milk. What good is there in milk, I ask you? Nothing but dishwater! You'd die of a diet like that!… If I start trying to persuade him, all he does is laugh and make fun of me… No, he doesn't care for our food, that dear brother of mine!"

Our evenings were much more fun than the days. When the sun was setting and long shadows stretched across the courtyard, we – that is, Tatyana Ivanovna, Pobedimsky and I – would already be sitting on the steps outside the hut. We wouldn't talk until it got quite dark. What were we supposed to talk about, anyway, when we'd already said all there was to be said? There was only one bit of news, my uncle's arrival, but even that topic was soon exhausted. My tutor never took his eyes off Tatyana Ivanovna's face, and heaved deep sighs… At the time I didn't understand his sighs, nor look for an explanation, but now I find they explain a great deal.

When the shadows on the ground merged into one continuous shadow, Fyodor the bailiff would return from hunting or from the fields. This Fyodor struck me as a wild and even frightening man. He was the son of a Russianized gypsy from Izyum, swarthy, with big dark eyes, curly hair and a ragged beard; our local peasants at Kochuyevka only ever called him "that devil". There was a lot of the gypsy about him, quite apart from his appearance. He couldn't stand staying at home, and would disappear for days on end hunting or out in the fields. He was gloomy, ill-humoured, taciturn, afraid of no one, and recognized no one's authority over him. He was rude to my mother, spoke familiarly to me and despised Pobedimsky's learning. But Mother liked him because, despite his gypsy nature, he was scrupulously honest and hard-working. He loved his Tatyana Ivanovna passionately, like a gypsy, but this love of his expressed itself as moroseness and suffering. He never caressed his wife in front of us, but just goggled crossly at her and twisted his mouth in a grimace.

When he came in from the fields he would bang his gun down angrily on the floor of the hut, join us outside, and sit down next to his wife. After resting a little he would ask his wife some questions about household matters, and then lapse into silence again.

"Let's have a song," I would suggest.

My tutor would tune his guitar and strike up "In the Green Valley" in the gruff bass voice of a lay clerk. We would all join in the singing, the tutor in his bass, Fyodor in an almost inaudible light tenor, and I singing a descant in unison with Tatyana Ivanovna.

When all the sky was covered with stars, and the frogs had fallen silent, our supper would be brought over from the kitchen. We would go into the hut to eat. The tutor and the gypsy ate voraciously, making cracking noises which might have been bones crunching or their jaws snapping; Tatyana Ivanovna and I had our work cut out to secure our own shares. After supper the hut was plunged in deep sleep.

One day in late May we were sitting outside the hut waiting for our supper. Suddenly a shadow passed, and Gundasov appeared before us as if he had risen up through the ground. He gazed at us for a long time, then held up his hands and burst into merry laughter.

"Idyllic!" he said. "Singing and dreaming in the moon-light! How lovely, upon my soul! Can I sit and dream with you?"

We exchanged looks but said nothing. My uncle sat down on the bottom step, yawned and looked up at the sky. There was a silence. Pobedimsky, who had long been hoping to have a conversation with a fresh face, was pleased with his luck and was the first to break the silence. He only had one topic for intellectual conversations – epizootics. It sometimes happens that when you find yourself in a crowd of thousands of people, for some reason only one physiognomy among those thousands carves itself a permanent place in your memory. It was the same with Pobedimsky: out of everything he had been told in his half year at the veterinary institute, there was only one fact he had committed to memory:

"Epizootics cause enormous damage to our nation's agriculture. In the battle against them, society must act hand in hand with the government."

Before saying this to Gundasov, my tutor coughed three times and anxiously wrapped his cape tightly about him, repeating the gesture several times over. On being told about epizootics, my uncle stared hard at the tutor and snorted with laughter.

"That's nice, upon my soul..." he muttered, looking us up and down as if we were shop dummies. "That's exactly what life's about... That's what real life is supposed to be like. And you, Pelageya Ivanovna, why don't you say anything?" he went on, turning to Tatyana Ivanovna.

She coughed in embarrassment.

"Carry on talking, gentlemen, sing... and play! Don't waste any time. That villain, Time, is running on, he won't wait for you! Upon my soul, before you've had time to look around you, old age will be upon you... And then it'll be too late to live! That's how it is, Pelageya Ivanovna... No sense just sitting there and saying nothing..."

At that point our supper was brought over from the kitchen. My uncle came into the hut to keep us company, and ate five curd cheese pastries and a duck wing. As he ate, he watched us. He found us all delightful and touching. Whatever rubbish my dear tutor came out with, whatever Tatyana Ivanovna did, everything was sweet and charming. After supper, when Tatyana Ivanovna sat modestly down in the corner and picked up her knitting, he never took his eyes off her little hands, while chattering away non-stop.

"You, my friends, have got to hurry up and start living, as quick as you can…" he said. "God forbid that you sacrifice the present for the sake of the future! Youth, health, ardour, are all in the present; the future is nothing but smoke and deception! The day you hit twenty, you have to start to live."

Tatyana Ivanovna dropped a needle. My uncle leapt up, picked up the needle and handed it to her with a bow. That was when I first realized that some people were even more refined than Pobedimsky.

"Yes…" my uncle went on. "Love, and get married… and play the fool. Folly is far more alive and healthy than all our efforts as we strive for a rational life."

My uncle talked a great deal, for a long time, so long that we got bored with him. I sat on a box to one side, listening to him and dozing. I was tormented by the fact that in all this time he hadn't once taken any notice of me. He left the hut at two in the morning, by which time I had succumbed to drowsiness and fallen fast asleep.

From then on my uncle began visiting our hut every evening. He joined in our singing, ate supper and stayed on till two in the morning every time, relentlessly chattering on, always about the same thing. He gave up working in the evenings and at night, and by the end of June, when he had learnt how to eat Mother's turkeys and fruit compotes, he gave up daytime work as well. He tore himself away from his work table and threw himself into "life". By day he would stride around the garden, whistling at the farmhands and getting in the way of their work, forcing them to tell him all their various histories. When he caught sight of Tatyana Ivanovna, he would run up to her, and if she was carrying something he'd offer his help, to her great embarrassment.

The longer the summer went on, the more frivolous, fidgety and absent-minded my dear uncle became. Pobedimsky was greatly disappointed in him.

"He has a one-track mind…" he said. "There's nothing in the least to show that he's in the top echelons of the administration. He doesn't even know how to talk. Every other word he says is 'upon my soul'. No, I don't like him!"

From then on, when my uncle came to visit our hut, Fyodor and my tutor showed a noticeable change in their behaviour. Fyodor stopped going out to hunt, came home early, became even more taciturn, and seemed to glare particularly savagely at his wife. My tutor stopped talking about epizootics in my uncle's presence, looked sulky, and even wore a scornful smile.

"Here comes our mousy little colt!" he once muttered when my uncle was on his way over to our hut.

I accounted for the change in these two men by deciding that they felt offended by my uncle. The absent-minded man would muddle up their names; right up to his departure, he never managed to work out which one of them was the tutor and which was Tatyana Ivanovna's husband. And Tatyana Ivanovna herself he sometimes called Nastasya, sometimes Pelageya, or Yevdokia. Filled with tender delight at us, he laughed and treated us like little children... All that, of course, could have offended the young people. But it wasn't a question of offence, as I later discovered, but of more delicate feelings.

On one of those evenings, I remember, I was sitting on my box and struggling to stay awake. A stickiness had settled on my eyes, and my body, worn out by running around all day, was sagging to one side. But I was fighting against sleep, and trying to watch. It was around midnight. Tatyana Ivanovna, rosy-faced and demure as ever, was sitting at a little table, stitching a shirt for her husband. Fyodor was glaring at her from one corner, sulky and morose, while in the other corner sat Pobedimsky, sinking down into the high collar of his tunic and sniffing crossly. My uncle was pacing back and forth around the room, thinking about something. Silence reigned; the only sound to be heard was the rustle of linen in Tatyana Ivanovna's hands. Suddenly my uncle stopped in front of Tatyana Ivanovna and said:

"You're all so young and fresh and good-looking, and you lead such untroubled lives in the midst of this quiet – I really envy you. I've become attached to this life of yours; my heart aches when I remember that I have to leave… Believe me, I mean what I say!"

My eyelids drooped with weariness, and I knew no more. A thump of some kind woke me, and I saw my uncle standing in front of Tatyana Ivanovna, gazing tenderly at her. His cheeks were flushed.

"My life has been wasted," he said. "I've never had a life! Your young face reminds me of my lost youth – I'd be willing to stay here looking at you till the day I die. I'd love to take you to Petersburg with me."

"What for?" demanded Fyodor hoarsely.

"I'd stand her on my desk in a glass case to admire her, and show her off to other people. You know, Pelageya Ivanovna, we don't have women like you back there. We have rich ones, and noble ones, and a few beautiful ones, but there's none of this genuine life… this healthy serenity…"

My uncle sat down facing Tatyana Ivanovna and took her by the hand.

"So you won't come to Petersburg with me?" he laughed. "At least give me your hand to take with me, then… What a lovely little hand! Can't I take it? Oh you mean thing, let me kiss it at least…"

Suddenly there came the loud creak of a chair. Fyodor sprang to his feet and walked up to his wife with heavy, measured steps. His face was greyish pale and shaking.

With a swing of his arm he banged his fist hard down on the table, saying hoarsely:

"I won't have it!"

At that same moment Pobedimsky, too, leapt up from his chair. Pale with fury, he went up to Tatyana Ivanovna and also banged his fist on the table...

"I... I won't have it!" he said.

"What? What's up?" asked my uncle in astonishment.

"I won't have it!" repeated Fyodor, banging the table again.

My uncle jumped to his feet and blinked nervously. He was on the point of saying something, but was too startled and frightened to bring out a single word. With an embarrassed smile, he shuffled out of the hut like an old man, leaving his hat behind. When, shortly after that, my mother ran into the hut in alarm, Fyodor and Pobedimsky were still banging their fists on the table like a pair of blacksmiths with their hammers, repeating "I won't have it!"

"What's going on here?" asked Mother. "Why has my brother been taken ill? What's up?"

One look at Tatyana Ivanovna's pale, terrified face and her husband's blind fury was probably enough for her to guess. She heaved a sigh and shook her head.

"That'll do, that's quite enough thumping the table!" she said. "Stop it, Fyodor! And what are you banging it for, Yegor Alexeyevich? What's it to do with you?"

Pobedimsky came to his senses and looked embarrassed. Fyodor stared intently at him, then at his wife, and started pacing about the room. When my mother had left the hut I saw something which afterwards I believed for a long time had been a dream. I saw Fyodor grab hold of my tutor, lift him in the air and hurl him out of the door…

When I awoke next morning the tutor's bed was empty. I asked the nurse where he was and she whispered that he'd been carried off to hospital early that morning with a broken arm. Remembering yesterday's row, I was upset by the news, and went outside. It was a grey day. Clouds covered the sky, and dust, scraps of paper and feathers were blowing about in the wind… You could feel rain not far off. The people and the animals all looked dejected. When I entered the house, I was told not to tramp around because my mother was in bed with a migraine. What was I going to do? I went out of the gate, sat down on a bench and tried to make sense of all I had seen and heard the day before. A road ran down from our gate, past the forge and a puddle that never dried out, to join the main post road… I looked at the telegraph poles, with clouds of dust eddying about them, and the sleepy birds perched on the telegraph wires, and suddenly I felt so depressed that I burst into tears.

A dusty wagonette crammed full of townspeople drove by along the main road; they were probably on their way to the shrine. No sooner had it disappeared from sight than a light carriage and pair appeared, carrying our police inspector Akim Nikitich, who was standing up and holding on to the coachman's belt. To my great surprise, the carriage swung into our drive and flew past me into the gates. As I stood there wondering why the police inspector had shown up, there was another noise, and a troika came into view trotting along the road. In that carriage stood the district police chief, pointing our gates out to his driver.

"And what's this one come for?" I wondered, looking at the police chief all covered with dust. "Pobedimsky must have complained to the police about Fyodor and now they've come to carry him off to prison."

But the riddle wasn't that simple. The inspector and his chief were just the advance guard; no more than five minutes later, a carriage drove in through our gates, flashing past me so quickly that all I could glimpse through the window was a ginger beard.

Lost in surmises, and with an ominous feeling that all was not well, I ran to the house. The first person I saw in the hallway was my mother. She was pale and horror-struck, watching a door through which men's voices could be heard. The visitors had taken her by surprise at the height of her migraine.

"Who's come, Mama?" I asked.

"Sister!" came my uncle's voice. "Serve us up a bite, the Governor and me!"

"A bite! Easy to say!" whispered my mother, sinking with dread. "Whatever can I manage to prepare on the spot? Put to shame in my old age!"

Clutching her head, she rushed into the kitchen. The unannounced arrival of the Governor had galvanized and overwhelmed everyone in the place. A merciless slaughter began. A dozen chickens were killed, five turkeys and eight ducks. Our old gander, Mother's favourite and the forefather of our whole flock of geese, got beheaded in the confusion. The coachmen and the cook went mad and slaughtered birds right and left, paying no regard to their age or breed. For the sake of some sauce or other, a pair of my precious tumbler pigeons perished, though I loved them as dearly as Mother had loved her gander. It was a long time before I forgave the Governor for their deaths.

That evening, when the Governor and his retinue, after their lavish dinner, took their seats in their carriages and drove away, I went into the house to look at the remains of the banquet. Peeping into the drawing room from the hallway, I saw my uncle and my mother. My uncle, hands behind his back, was pacing irritably back and forth by the wall, shrugging his shoulders. Mother, exhausted and looking much thinner than before, was sitting on the divan and following her brother's movements with heavy eyes.

"I'm sorry, sister, but it won't do…" grumbled my uncle with a scowl. "I present the Governor to you, and you don't even offer him your hand! He was quite put out, poor man!

It's just not good enough… Simplicity is all very well, but there are limits… upon my soul… And then that dinner! How can you serve a dinner like that? I mean, what was that mess you served up for the fourth course?"

"That was duck in a sweet sauce…" replied Mother softly.

"Duck… I'm sorry, sister, but… but now I've got heartburn! I'm ill!"

He put on a sour, tearful face and went on:

"Why the devil did that Governor have to turn up! Much I needed him here! Blp… got heartburn! I won't be able to sleep, or work… I'm in a mess… And I don't see how you can all live here, doing no work… in this deadly boring place! Now I've got a pain coming on in the pit of my stomach!…"

He scowled and paced about a bit faster.

"Brother," my mother asked softly, "how much would it cost for you to go abroad?"

"Not less than three thousand…" my uncle said tearfully. "I'd go, but where am I to find the money? I haven't a kopek! Blp… got heartburn!"

He stopped still, looked miserably up at the window and the overcast grey sky outside, and started pacing about again.

There was a silence… Mother looked at the icon for a long time, thinking something over, then started crying, and said:

"I'll give you the three thousand, brother…"

Three days later the majestic trunks were despatched to the station, and the Privy Councillor drove off after them. Taking leave of my mother, he wept, and for a long time couldn't remove his lips from her hand. But when he got into the carriage, his face lit up with childish joy… Radiantly happy, he settled himself down comfortably, kissed his hand in farewell to my weeping mother, and then suddenly and unexpectedly rested his eyes on me. A look of absolute astonishment spread over his face.

"And who's this lad?" he asked.

My mother, who had assured me that my uncle had been sent to us by God as a stroke of luck for me, was utterly mortified by this question. But I was in no mood for questions. I looked at my uncle's happy face, and for some reason felt terribly sorry for him. I couldn't stop myself jumping up into his carriage and tightly hugging this frivolous man, weak as all men are. Looking into his eyes and wishing to say something nice to him, I asked him:

"Uncle, have you ever been in a war?"

"Ah, dear boy…" laughed my uncle, giving me a kiss. "Such a dear boy, upon my soul. How natural, how full of life this all is… upon my soul…"

The carriage moved off… I watched it go, and that parting "upon my soul" stayed with me a long time.

# THE KISS

AT EIGHT O'CLOCK on the evening of 20th May, all six batteries of the N—— Reserve Artillery Brigade stopped for the night in the village of Mestechki, en route for their encampment. At the height of the general commotion, with some officers busying themselves around the guns while others gathered in the square by the church railings to listen to the billeting officers, a rider in civilian dress emerged from behind the church, riding a peculiar horse. It was a small dun-coloured animal with a fine neck and a short tail. Instead of walking straight ahead, it seemed to sidle along, performing little dancing movements with its legs as though they were being whipped. Coming up to the officers, the horseman raised his hat and said:

"His Excellency Lieutenant-General Von Rabbeck, the landowner here, invites the officers to come and drink tea with him this minute…"

The horse bowed its head, did a little dance and sidled backwards; the rider raised his hat once more, and an instant later he and his strange horse had vanished behind the church.

"What the devil!" grumbled some of the officers as they walked off to their billets. "What we want to do is sleep, and here's this Von Rabbeck and his tea party! We know what sort of a tea we'll get!"

The officers from all six batteries well remembered the occasion during manoeuvres last year, when they, along with the officers of a Cossack regiment, had been invited to tea in just the same way by a certain count, a local landowner and retired army officer. The hospitable and genial count had made much of them, laid on food and drink, and wouldn't let them go back to their billets in the village, but had them stay the night. That was all very well, of course, one couldn't have asked for better, but the trouble was that this old soldier got quite carried away by his young guests, kept them up till dawn telling them stories about his distinguished past, guided them all over the house, showed them his valuable paintings and his old engravings and antique weapons, read them out handwritten letters from important people, while the officers, shattered with exhaustion, listened and looked and longed for their beds, furtively yawning into their sleeves. By the time their host let them go, it was too late for bed.

Was Von Rabbeck another of that sort? Whether he was or not, there was no help for it. The officers changed, smartened up and set out en masse to find this landowner's home. On the square by the church they were told that they could get to his Excellency's by the lower path, going down behind the church to the river and following the riverbank all the way to his garden, where the garden paths would lead them the rest of the way; or by the upper path, straight down the road from the church, which would end up at the estate barns half a mile from the village. The officers decided to go the upper way.

"Who's this Von Rabbeck?" they wondered as they walked. "Is he the one who commanded the N—— cavalry division at Plevna?"

"No, that wasn't Von Rabbeck, he was just Rabbe, with no 'von'."

"Isn't this great weather!"

The road reached the first of the estate barns and branched into two. One branch led straight on till it vanished in the evening shadows, the other went to the right, towards the manor. The officers took the right turn and talked more quietly... The road was lined on either side by stone barns with red roofs, heavy and forbidding structures that looked very much like the barracks of a district town. Ahead of them were the lit windows of the manor house.

"Gentlemen – here's a good sign!" said one of the officers. "Our setter is running ahead of us all: that means he scents game!"

Leading the party was Lieutenant Lobytko, a tall, thick-set officer without the shadow of a moustache (he was over twenty-five, but his plump round face for some reason still showed no sign of a hair growth). He was renowned in the brigade for his sixth sense and ability to detect the presence of females at a distance. Now he turned back to his fellows and said:

"Yes, there must be women here. My instinct tells me so."

The officers were greeted on the threshold by Von Rabbeck in person. He was a good-looking elderly man of about sixty, dressed in civilian clothes. He shook hands with all his guests, told them that he was delighted, very happy to see them, but begged them most sincerely in God's name to forgive him for not asking them to stay the night. Two of his sisters with their children, and some brothers and some neighbours of his, were visiting, so there wasn't a spare bed in the house.

The general shook everybody's hand, and begged pardon, and smiled – but his face clearly showed that he was by no means as pleased to see his guests as last year's count had been, and the only reason he had invited the officers was that he believed good manners demanded it. And the officers themselves, as they climbed the thickly carpeted stairs and listened to him talking, felt that the only reason they had been asked to this house was that the general felt he couldn't get out of it. And when the officers saw the footmen hurrying to light the lamps downstairs by the entrance and upstairs in the hall, they began to feel that they had brought trouble and alarm into this home. If, as it seemed, there was some sort of family celebration going on, bringing in two sisters with their children, and some brothers and neighbours too, how could anybody want to be saddled with nineteen unknown officers?

Upstairs, at the entrance to the drawing room, the guests were greeted by a tall, graceful, elderly lady with dark eyebrows on a long face, bearing a marked resemblance to the Empress Eugénie. Smiling cordially and majestically, she said that she was happy and delighted to welcome her guests, and apologized for the fact that she and her husband were prevented from inviting the officers to stay the night with them on this occasion. Her attractive, majestic smile, which instantly vanished from her face whenever something caused her to turn away from her guests, made it clear that she had come across a great many officers in her day, and at present couldn't be bothered with them, and that if she had invited them to her home and was now apologizing to them, that was because her breeding and social position demanded it.

The officers entered the great dining room to find a dozen ladies and gentlemen, old and young, sitting at one end of a long table drinking tea. Behind their chairs a group of men could be discerned through a haze of cigar smoke. One of them, a lanky young man with ginger side whiskers and a lisp, was standing talking about something very loudly in English. Through a doorway beyond this group, a bright room with pale-blue furnishings could be seen.

"Gentlemen, there are so many of you, I can't possibly introduce you all!" the general announced loudly, trying to sound very light-hearted. "Please just make yourselves known to each other!"

The officers, some wearing very serious or even stern expressions, others with forced smiles, but all feeling extremely awkward, made their bows as best they could and sat down to drink tea.

The most uncomfortable of them all was Captain Ryabovich. He was a small, round-shouldered, bespectacled officer with whiskers like a lynx's. While some of his comrades were putting on serious faces and others wore forced smiles, his own face with its lynx-like whiskers and spectacles seemed to say "I'm the shyest, most modest and colourless officer in the whole brigade!" At first, when he entered the dining room and then sat at tea, he couldn't focus his attention on any single person or thing. The faces, the dresses, the cut-glass brandy decanters, the steam from the tea glasses, the moulded cornices – everything melted into a single overwhelming impression that filled him with alarm and made him long to hide his face. Like a man giving his first public reading in front of an audience, he could see everything that lay before his eyes, but found it difficult to make sense of what he saw (physiologists describe this state, in which the subject can see without understanding what he sees, as "psychical blindness"). After a short while, once he got used to his surroundings, Ryabovich began to understand what he was seeing, and set about observing it. As a shy, withdrawn person, he was immediately struck by a quality he himself had always lacked – the astonishing boldness of his new acquaintances. Von Rabbeck, his wife, two elderly ladies, a young girl in a lilac dress, and the young man with ginger side whiskers who turned out to be Von Rabbeck's younger son, very cunningly disposed themselves among the officers – quite as if they had rehearsed the move – and immediately started up a heated argument; the guests were obliged to join in… The girl in lilac argued vehemently that artillerymen had a far easier life than men in the cavalry or infantry, while Von Rabbeck and the elderly ladies maintained the contrary. There was a heated exchange of views. Ryabovich watched the girl in lilac arguing with intense feeling about something quite remote and devoid of interest to her, and observed the insincere smiles appearing on her face and vanishing again.

Skilfully, Von Rabbeck and his family drew the officers into the argument, while themselves keeping a careful eye on their drinking glasses and their mouths to see if they were drinking up, and if they were enjoying it, and why such and such wasn't eating any biscuits or drinking any brandy. And the longer Ryabovich watched and listened, the more he liked this insincere but beautifully disciplined family.

After tea the officers went through to the drawing room. Lobytko's sixth sense hadn't let him down: there were plenty of girls and young ladies there. The lieutenant himself, the "setter", was already standing beside a very young blonde girl in a black dress. Bending forward in a dashing posture, as though leaning on an invisible sabre, he was smiling and gesturing flirtatiously with his shoulders. He must have been telling her something very boring and pointless, because she looked condescendingly at his plump face and said "Really?" in a voice devoid of interest. That bored "Really?" could have told the setter, had he been wiser, that he wasn't likely to be told "Go fetch!"

The piano struck up; a melancholy waltz wafted out of the wide-open windows, and for some reason everybody was reminded that outside it was spring, a May evening. Everybody caught the scent of young poplar leaves, and roses, and lilac. Ryabovich, moved by the music and the brandy he had drunk, looked at the window out of the corner of his eye, smiled, watched the women moving around, and felt that the scent of roses, poplars and lilac was coming not from the garden but from the ladies' faces and gowns.

Von Rabbeck's son asked a skinny-looking girl to dance, and did a couple of turns round the room with her. Lobytko, gliding over the parquet floor, flew up to the girl in lilac and carried her off around the room. The dancing had started… Ryabovich stood near the door, among those who were not dancing, and watched. In all his life, he had never once danced; never in his life had he held his arm round the waist of a respectable woman.

He loved to see a man putting his arm round the waist of a girl he didn't know, and offering her his shoulder to rest her hand, all in full view of everybody; but he was quite unable to imagine himself in that man's situation. There had been a time when he envied his comrades their courage and quick-wittedness, and suffered spiritual agonies; the consciousness that he was shy, round-shouldered and colourless, with a long waist and whiskers like a lynx, used to make him deeply unhappy; but with the passing years he had got used to this feeling, and now, gazing at the people dancing or talking together in loud voices, he no longer felt envious. He just felt rather touched and sad.

When the quadrille started, young Von Rabbeck came up to the group of people who were not dancing and invited two officers to a game of billiards. The officers accepted and left the room with him. With nothing else to do, Ryabovich wandered off after them, hoping to play some part at least in the evening's activities. They went from the drawing room to the parlour, thence into a narrow glass-lined corridor, and from there into another room where the figures of three sleepy footmen leapt up from a sofa as soon as they appeared. Eventually, after passing through a whole series of rooms, young Von Rabbeck and the officers entered a small room with a billiard table. They began to play.

Ryabovich had never played any game but cards. He stood by the billiard table and watched the players without interest. They had unbuttoned their frock coats and were striding around, cues in hand, swapping puns and shouting out words he couldn't understand. They took no notice of him, except that from time to time one of them would accidentally brush an elbow against him or jog him with a cue, then turn and say "Pardon!" Before the first frame was even over, Ryabovich was feeling bored, unwanted and in the way… He longed to be back in the drawing room, and walked out.

On his way back, he met with a little adventure. When he had got halfway he realized that he had taken a wrong turning. He clearly remembered that he was supposed to come across the figures of three sleepy footmen, but although he had passed through five or six rooms, these figures seemed to have vanished through the floor. As soon as he realized his mistake, he went back a bit, took a right turn, and found himself in a dimly lit little room he hadn't seen on his way to the billiard room. He stood here for a moment, then tentatively opened the first door he could see and entered a room that was quite dark. Straight ahead was the crack of a doorway with bright light shining through, and the faint sounds of a melancholy mazurka being played beyond the door. As in the drawing room, the windows around him were wide open, bringing a scent of poplars, lilac and roses…

Ryabovich paused in thought… At that moment he was startled by the sound of scurrying footsteps and the rustle of a gown, and a female voice breathlessly whispered "At last!" A pair of soft, fragrant, unmistakably female arms were clasped round his neck, a warm cheek was pressed against his, and at the same moment there was the sound of a kiss. But straight away the giver of the kiss uttered a little shriek and, as it seemed to Ryabovich, recoiled from him in disgust. He too almost cried out, and ran towards the bright crack in the doorway...

When he reached the drawing room his heart was pounding and his hands trembling so visibly that he hastened to hide them behind his back. At first he was tormented by embarrassment, dreading that everyone in the room knew that he had just been embraced and kissed by a woman; he cringed and looked uneasily from side to side; but once he had reassured himself that everyone in the room was still happily dancing and chatting as before, he surrendered himself to a new sensation which he had never previously experienced in his life. Something strange was happening to him... His neck, so recently embraced by a pair of soft and fragrant arms, seemed to have been anointed with oil. His cheek, next to his left moustache, where the stranger had kissed him, tingled with a faint but pleasant chill, like mint drops, and the more he rubbed the place, the stronger he felt the chill. The whole of his body, from his head to his heels, was filled with a new and strange sensation, which was growing more and more intense... He felt like skipping about, talking, running out into the garden, laughing out loud… He forgot all about being round-shouldered and colourless, and having lynx-like whiskers and an "indefinite sort of look" (that was how his appearance had once been described, in a ladies' conversation which he had happened to overhear). When Von Rabbeck's wife walked past him, he gave her such a broad, friendly smile that she stopped and looked enquiringly at him.

"I absolutely love your home!" he told her, straightening his glasses.

The general's wife smiled and said that the house had belonged to her father. Then she asked him whether his own parents were alive, and whether he had been long in the army, and why he was so thin, and so on… Having received replies to all her questions, she moved on, while his smile grew even friendlier after this conversation, and he began to think that he was surrounded by splendid people…

At dinner Ryabovich mechanically ate and drank everything he was offered, and heard nothing, as he tried to make sense of the adventure he had just had… This adventure had a mysterious and romantic feel to it, but explaining it was easy. No doubt one of the young girls or married ladies had arranged an assignation in that dark room, had been waiting there a long time, and in her nervous excitement had taken Ryabovich for her swain. That was all the more likely since Ryabovich, on his way through the darkened room, had paused in thought, so that he looked like a man who was also awaiting something... That was how Ryabovich accounted for the kiss he had received.

"But who is she?" he wondered, looking at the ladies' faces. "She must be young, because elderly ladies don't make assignations. And she's a cultured person, you could tell that from the rustle of her dress, her scent, her voice..."

He rested his glance on the girl in lilac, and very much liked the look of her. She had beautiful shoulders and arms, an intelligent face and a lovely voice. Looking at her, Ryabovich wanted his stranger to have been her and no one else... But then she gave a kind of false laugh, and wrinkled her long nose which he thought made her look old. So he moved on to look at the blonde girl in black. She was younger, with a simpler and more sincere look, and she had a lovely forehead and was drinking very prettily out of her glass. Now Ryabovich wanted her to be the one. But soon he found that her face was too flat, and shifted his gaze to her neighbour...

"It's hard to guess," he said, musing. "If you just take the lilac one's shoulders and arms, and add the blonde's forehead, and take the eyes from the one on Lobytko's left, then..."

He combined all these features together in his mind, and came up with an image of the girl who had kissed him. It was the image that he wanted, but he couldn't manage to find it at the table...

After dinner the well-fed and rather tipsy guests began taking their leave and thanking their hosts. The hosts once again started apologizing for being unable to put them up for the night.

"I'm very, very glad to know you, gentlemen!" said the general, sincerely this time (probably because people are far more sincere and friendly to their departing guests than to those just arriving). "Very glad! Come and see us on your way back! No standing on ceremony! Which way are you going? Do you want to go by the upper way? No, go through the garden, take the lower way – it's shorter from here."

The officers passed out into the garden. After the bright lights and the noise, they found the garden very dark and quiet. They walked in silence all the way to the gate. They were half drunk, light-hearted and pleased with everything, but the darkness and silence made them thoughtful for a space. Each of them probably wondered, as Ryabovich did, whether the time would ever come when they too would be like Von Rabbeck, with a big house, a family and a garden; whether they too would ever have the opportunity of welcoming guests – even insincerely – and feeding them lavishly, and making them tipsy and contented?

As they walked out of the gate, they all immediately began talking and laughing out loud, for no reason. Now they were following a path which went down to the river and then ran along by the waterside, skirting the bushes on the bank, the runnels and the willows overhanging the water. The path and the riverbank were hard to make out, and the opposite bank was lost in the gloom. Here and there a star would be reflected, shimmering and dissolving in the dark water; that was the only thing to show that the river was running fast. It was very quiet there. Sleepy curlews were calling on the far bank, while a nightingale in a bush on the near bank was trilling at full voice, taking no notice whatever of the crowd of officers. They stopped by the bush, and touched it, but the nightingale went on singing.

"What about that!" came the admiring voices. "Here we are, right next to him, and he's not taking a blind bit of notice! What a rascal!"

At the end of the riverside stretch, the path led upwards to open out onto the roadway near the church fence. Here the officers sat down, tired after their climb, to rest and smoke. A dim red flame showed on the far bank, and they idly wondered whether it was a bonfire, or a fire seen through a house window, or something different... Ryabovich, too, gazed at the fire; it seemed to be smiling and winking at him, as though it knew all about the kiss.

When he returned to his quarters, Ryabovich quickly undressed and got into bed. He was sharing the hut with Lobytko and Lieutenant Merzlyakov, a peaceable, untalkative young man who had the reputation among his fellows of being well educated, always carrying a copy of the

*European Herald* with him, and reading it whenever he got a chance. Lobytko undressed and spent a long time pacing the room with a dissatisfied air, before sending his orderly out for some beer. Merzlyakov went to bed, stood a candle by the bedhead and immersed himself in the *European Herald*.

"Who can she be?" wondered Ryabovich, gazing at the soot on the ceiling.

His neck still felt as if it had been anointed with oil, and there was a chill like mint drops beside his mouth. The lilac girl's shoulders and arms, the forehead and honest eyes of the blonde in black, and other waists, dresses, brooches, all drifted through his imagination. He tried to fix his attention on these images, but they danced about and dissolved and flickered before him. When all the images completely disappeared, merging into the broad black background that you always see when you shut your eyes, Ryabovich began to hear hurried footsteps, the rustle of a dress, the sound of a kiss – and he was overcome by intense, unreasoning happiness... As he submitted to it, he heard the orderly return and report that there was no beer to be had. Lobytko was quite outraged and started pacing about the room again.

"Well, isn't he an ass!" he exclaimed, pausing now by Ryabovich, now by Merzlyakov. "What a fool, what an imbecile a man must be, not to find any beer! Eh? Well, I ask you, isn't he a villain?"

"Of course you won't find any beer here," remarked Merzlyakov, without raising his eyes from the *European Herald*.

"Really? You think not?" insisted Lobytko. "Good God, if you dumped me on the moon, I'd find you beer on the spot, and women too! I'll go off and find some right away… Call me a scoundrel if I don't!"

He spent a long time dressing and pulling on his tall boots, finished his cigarette in silence and set off.

"Rabbeck, Grabbeck, Labbeck," he muttered, stopping in the outer room. "I don't feel like going on my own, damn it. Ryabovich, wouldn't you like to come for a stroll, eh?"

Getting no answer, he turned back, slowly undressed and put himself to bed. Merzlyakov heaved a sigh, put down the *European Herald* and blew out the candle.

"Mm-yes," muttered Lobytko, lighting a cigarette in the dark.

Ryabovich pulled the bedclothes over his head, rolled himself into a ball, and tried to gather together all the fleeting images in his mind's eye and unite them in a single whole. But nothing came of it. Soon he fell asleep, and his last thought was that someone had caressed him, and made him happy, and that something uncommon, silly, but extraordinarily good and joyful had come into his life. Even in his sleep, that thought never left him.

When he awoke, the sensations of oil on his neck and minty coolness near his lips had vanished, but waves of joy still washed over his heart just as they had the day before. He looked up in delight at the window frames, painted gold by the rising sun, and listened to the street sounds outside. A loud conversation was taking place outside the window. His battery commander, Lebedetsky, who had just caught up with his brigade, was talking with his sergeant major in a very loud voice (being unaccustomed to talking quietly).

"What else?" shouted the commander.

"When they were shoeing the horses yesterday, your Honour, they drove a nail into Pigeon's foot. The vet's orderly applied clay and vinegar. They're leading him on his own for now. And another thing, your Honour, Artificer Artemyev got drunk yesterday and his lieutenant ordered him carried on the limber of a spare gun carriage."

The sergeant major further reported that Karpov had forgotten the new lanyards for the trumpets and also the tent pegs, and that the officers had spent the previous evening as guests of General Von Rabbeck. During this conversation, the red-bearded face of Lebedetsky appeared at the window. He screwed up his short-sighted eyes to look at the officers' sleepy faces, and bade them good morning.

"All well here?" he asked.

"The pole saddle horse has a sore shoulder from the new collar."

The commander sighed, thought a bit, and said in a loud voice:

"I'm just thinking of dropping in on Alexandra Yevgrafovna. I have to pay her a visit. Well, carry on. I'll catch up with you tonight."

A quarter of an hour later the brigade set off. As it moved along the road past the general's barns, Ryabovich glanced sideways at the house. The windows were shuttered – evidently everyone there was still asleep. And the girl who had kissed him last night was sleeping too. He tried to imagine her asleep. Her bedroom window wide open, branches with green leaves looking in, the morning freshness, the scent of poplars, lilac and roses, the bed, the chair with her dress on it, the dress that had rustled last night, her little slippers, her little watch on the table – he could see it all clearly and distinctly, but her own features, her enchanting sleepy smile, those very things that were important and special about her – they eluded his imagination, as quicksilver slips away under one's finger. A quarter of a mile further on, he looked back. The yellow church, the house, the river and the garden were bathed in sunshine; the river between its bright green banks, reflecting the blue sky and glinting silver here and there in the sunlight, was a very lovely sight. Ryabovich cast a last look at Mestechki and felt very sad, as though parting from something he held very close and dear.

On the road, after that, there was nothing to be seen but the familiar, boring scenes... To the right and left were fields of young rye and buckwheat, with rooks hopping about. Look ahead and all you see is dust and the backs of men's heads, look back and you see the same dust and faces... Ahead of the column, four men with sabres are marching – they're the vanguard. Behind them, a crowd of singers, and behind the singers, trumpeters on horseback. The vanguard and the singers, like torchbearers in a funeral cortège, keep forgetting to maintain the regulation distance, and run on a long way ahead... Ryabovich is with the first cannon of the fifth battery. He can see all four batteries ahead of him. For a non-military man, this long, cumbersome procession of a brigade on the move looks like a strange, incomprehensible jumble; you have no idea why a single cannon has so many men around it, and why it's being drawn by so many horses, wearing a strange tangle of harness, as if the whole thing really was so dreadfully difficult. But Ryabovich understands it all, and so he finds it completely uninteresting. He learned long ago why the officer leading each battery has a sturdy bombardier riding by his side, and why he is called the leader; behind this bombardier he can see the horsemen of the first and then the middle units. Ryabovich knows that the horses on the left, on which they ride, are called saddle horses, while the ones on the right are the draught horses; that's all very uninteresting. Behind the rider come two pole horses. One of them carries a rider, whose back is covered with yesterday's dust, and who wears a clumsy-looking, very peculiar piece of wood on his right leg; Ryabovich knows the purpose of that bit of wood, and it doesn't seem odd to him. The mounted men, every one of them, mechanically wave their whips, and every now and then they shout out something. The cannon itself is an ugly thing. The limber is loaded with sacks of oats, covered with canvas, and the gun is festooned with kettles, soldiers' knapsacks and bags, so that it looks like a harmless little animal surrounded for no apparent reason by men and horses. On its downwind side, six men are marching and swinging their arms: they are the gunners. Behind this gun come more leaders, horsemen and pole horses, pulling along another cannon as ugly and unimpressive as the first. And a third one follows the second, and then a fourth; beside the fourth cannon rides an officer, and so forth. The brigade consists of six batteries in all, and each battery comprises four cannon. The column stretches for half a mile, with the baggage train bringing up the rear. Beside it, walking deep in thought, with his long-eared head drooping low, comes a very nice-looking beast – Magar the donkey, brought back from Turkey by one of the battery commanders.

Ryabovich looked indifferently ahead and behind him, at the backs of the men's heads and at their faces. At any other time he would have fallen into a doze, but now he was totally immersed in his new and pleasant thoughts. At first, when the brigade was just setting off, he wanted to persuade himself that the episode of the kiss could only be of interest as a mysterious little adventure; that it was a trivial occurrence, nothing more, and that taking it seriously would be at least stupid, if not worse. But soon he shrugged off all logic, and gave himself over to his dreams… He might picture himself in Von Rabbeck's drawing room, sitting next to a girl who looked like the one in lilac and the blonde in black; or he would close his eyes and see himself with a different girl, a complete stranger, with very indistinct features; in his imagination he talked with her, caressed her, rested his head on her shoulder, imagined war and separation, and then reunion, dinner with his wife, children…

"To your poles!" The command rang out every time they went downhill.

He, too, would call out "To your poles!", fearing that his shout might interrupt his dreams and recall him to the present…

Riding past some landowner's estate on the way, Ryabovich looked over the fence into its garden. He glimpsed a long avenue, straight as a ruler, surfaced with yellow sand and lined by young birch trees… As eagerly as a man in a dream, he imagined little feminine feet walking over the yellow sand, and quite unexpectedly his imagination called up a clear vision of the one who had kissed him, and whom he had managed to picture at dinner last night. That image stayed in his mind and would not leave him after that.

At noon there was a shout from the rear, by the baggage train:

"Steady! Eyes left! Officers!"

And the brigade general drove past in a carriage drawn by two white horses. He stopped beside the second battery and shouted something that no one could make out. A number of officers galloped up to him, Ryabovich among them.

"Well, how's it going? What?" asked the general, blinking with reddened eyes. "Any sick?"

On receiving answers to his questions, the general, a skinny little man, chewed and thought a bit, turned to one of the officers and said:

"The rider of one of the pole horses on the number three gun took off his leg guard and hung it on the limber, the swine. Have him punished."

Then he looked up at Ryabovich and continued:

"Your choke-straps look too long to me…"

After making a few more boring comments, the general looked at Lobytko with a grin.

"You're looking very glum today, Lieutenant Lobytko," he said. "Missing Lopukhova, are you? Eh? Gentlemen, he's pining for Lopukhova!"

Lopukhova was a very tall, plump lady, well beyond her fortieth year. The general, who had a fondness for large women, however old they were, suspected his officers of sharing his tastes. The officers smiled respectfully. Pleased with having said something very witty and cutting, the general gave a loud guffaw, touched his driver on the back and saluted. The carriage rolled on…

ANTON CHEKHOV

"Everything I dream about now, which all seems so unearthly and impossible to me at present, is actually very commonplace," thought Ryabovich, gazing at the clouds of dust rising behind the general's carriage. "It's all very ordinary, and everyone goes through it... That general, for instance, was in love once, and now he's married with children. Captain Wachter is married and beloved too, though the back of his head is very ugly and red and he has no waist... Salmanov is coarse and too much of a Tartar, but he had a love affair which ended in marriage... I'm just the same as everybody else, and sooner or later I'll have the same experience as everybody else..."

And the idea that he was an ordinary man, and living an ordinary life, cheered and consoled him. He could be as bold as he liked now, picturing *her* and his own happiness, with no constraint on his imagination...

When the brigade arrived at its destination that evening, and the officers were resting in their tents, Ryabovich, Merzlyakov and Lobytko sat around a box eating their supper. Merzlyakov ate without haste, chewing slowly and reading the *European Herald* on his knees. Lobytko talked non-stop and kept filling up his beer glass, while Ryabovich, his head confused from dreaming all day long, drank and said nothing. After three glasses he felt tipsy, weak and irresistibly impelled to share his new feelings with his comrades.

"An odd thing happened to me at those Rabbecks'..."

he began, trying to sound indifferent and ironical. "You know, I went to the billiard room…"

And he told the story of the kiss in great detail. A minute later he was done, and stopped talking… During that minute he had related everything, and he was terribly surprised to find that the story had taken so little time to tell. He had thought that he could have gone on telling about that kiss till morning. Having heard him out, Lobytko (who was a great liar, and therefore never believed anyone else) looked suspiciously at him and grinned. Merzlyakov raised his eyebrows, never taking his eyes off the *European Herald*, and said calmly:

"Extraordinary!… Throwing herself on a man's neck without saying anything… Must be off her head."

"Yes, I suppose she must…" agreed Ryabovich.

"The same sort of thing happened to me once…" said Lobytko, with a scared look. "I was on my way to Kovno last year… Took a second-class ticket… the carriage was full to bursting, and there was no chance of sleeping. I slipped the conductor half a rouble… He took my baggage and showed me to a compartment… I lay down and covered myself with a blanket… It was quite dark, you see. Suddenly I felt someone touching me on the shoulder and breathing in my face. I made a movement with my hand and felt someone's elbow… I opened my eyes, and just imagine – a woman! Dark eyes, lips as red as a prime salmon, nostrils dilated with passion, breasts like buffers…"

"Excuse me," Merzlyakov interrupted coolly. "I under-stand about the breasts, but how could you have seen her lips in the dark?"

Lobytko began prevaricating and laughing at Merzlyakov's slow-wittedness. It made Ryabovich wince. He walked away from the box, lay down and swore never to open his heart again.

Camp life began… One day followed another, all much the same. All this time Ryabovich felt, thought and behaved like a man in love. Every morning when the orderly brought him water to wash with, and he poured cold water over his head, he remembered that something good and warm had entered his life.

In the evenings, when his fellow officers began talking about love and women, he would listen to them, move closer, and wear the sort of expression that soldiers have when they listen to accounts of battles in which they themselves have taken part. And in the evenings when the tipsy officers went out on the town to play Don Juan, with the "setter" Lobytko at their head, Ryabovich, who took part in these excursions, invariably felt sad, deeply guilty, and mentally begged *her* for forgiveness… In his idle hours, or when lying awake at night, when he felt like remembering his childhood, his father and mother, and everything that was near and dear to him, he always remembered Mestechki too, and the strange horse, and Von Rabbeck and his wife who looked like Empress

Eugénie, and the dark room, and the bright crack in the doorway...

On 31st August he returned from camp, not with the whole brigade but just with two batteries. All the way he was in an anxious reverie, as though he was on his way home. He passionately wanted to see the peculiar horse again, and the church, and the insincere Von Rabbeck family, and that dark room. An "inner voice", which so often deceives lovers, somehow seemed to whisper to him that he was sure to see *her*... And he was tormented by all sorts of questions – how would he meet her? What would he talk about with her? Had she forgotten the kiss? At worst, he thought, even if he never met her, it would be nice for him just to walk through that dark room and remember...

That evening, the familiar church and white barns appeared on the horizon. Ryabovich's heart pounded... He took no notice of the officer riding beside him, who was telling him something; he forgot everything, and stared longingly at the river glistening in the distance, and the house roof, and the dovecote with doves circling above it in the light of the setting sun.

He rode up to the church and then listened to the billeting officers, expecting at any moment to see a horseman appear from beyond the fence and invite the officers to tea; but the billeting officers finished their briefing, the officers dismounted and strolled into the village, and no horseman appeared...

"Now Rabbeck will hear about our arrival from his peasants, and send someone for us," thought Ryabovich, entering his hut and not understanding why one fellow officer was lighting a candle, while the orderlies were hurriedly setting the samovars…

He became intensely anxious. He lay down, then got up and looked out of the window in case the horseman was on his way. But there was no horseman to be seen. He lay down again. Half an hour later he got up and, unable to bear the tension, went out and walked over to the church. The square by the church fence was dark and deserted… Three soldiers were standing by the downhill path, not talking. When they saw Ryabovich, they hastily drew themselves up and saluted. He returned their salute and started down along the path he remembered so well.

The whole sky over the far bank was bathed in crimson. The moon was rising. Two peasant women were moving about in a kitchen garden, talking in loud voices and picking cabbage leaves. Beyond the kitchen gardens, a few huts showed as dark shapes in the fields… On the near bank, everything was the same as last May: the path, the bushes, the willows overhanging the water… but now there was no sound from the bold nightingale, and no scent of poplars and young grass.

He went down to the river. Before him were the white shapes of the general's bath house and some bath sheets hanging on the parapet of a little bridge. He walked onto the bridge, stood there a moment, and quite needlessly fingered one of the sheets. It felt cold and rough. He looked down at the water... The river was running fast, gurgling almost inaudibly around the piles of the bath-house. The reddish moon was reflected in the water near the left bank; little ripples ran across its reflection, stretching it out, breaking it up, and looking as if they were trying to carry it away...

"How stupid! How stupid!" thought Ryabovich, gazing at the running water. "How pointless it all is!"

Now that he no longer expected anything, the story of the kiss, his impatience, his vague hopes and his disappointment appeared before him in a clear light. He no longer found it strange that he had given up on the general's horseman, and that he would never again see the girl who had accidentally kissed him instead of someone else. On the contrary, it would have been strange if he had seen her...

The water ran on, no one knew where or why. It was running just as it had in May. The water in May had run into a big river, from the river to the sea, then it had evaporated and turned into rain, and perhaps the very same water was now once more running past Ryabovich's eyes. What for? What was the point?

And the whole world, and the whole of life, appeared to Ryabovich to be an incomprehensible and pointless joke... Raising his eyes from the water and gazing up at the sky, he remembered once more how fate in the person of an unknown woman had accidentally caressed him; he remembered his summer dreams and imaginings; and his life seemed to him extraordinarily impoverished, shabby and colourless...

When he returned to his hut, he found none of his comrades there. The orderly reported that they had all gone off to visit "General Fon-tryabkin" who had sent a horseman to invite them... For a moment Ryabovich's heart leapt for joy; but he quelled it at once and put himself to bed. As if to spite his fate, as if he wanted to upset it, he did not go to the general's.

## PUSHKIN PRESS

Pushkin Press was founded in 1997, and publishes novels, essays, memoirs, children's books—everything from timeless classics to the urgent and contemporary.

This book is part of the Pushkin Collection of paperbacks, designed to be as satisfying as possible to hold and to enjoy. It is typeset in Monotype Baskerville, based on the transitional English serif typeface designed in the mid-eighteenth century by John Baskerville. It was litho-printed on Munken Premium White Paper and notch-bound by the independently owned printer TJ International in Padstow, Cornwall. The cover, with French flaps, was printed on Rives Linear Bright White paper. The paper and cover board are both acid-free and Forest Stewardship Council (FSC) certified.

Pushkin Press publishes the best writing from around the world—great stories, beautifully produced, to be read and read again.

STEFAN ZWEIG · EDGAR ALLAN POE · ISAAC BABEL
TOMÁS GONZÁLEZ · ULRICH PLENZDORF · JOSEPH KESSEL
VELIBOR ČOLIĆ · LOUISE DE VILMORIN · MARCEL AYMÉ
ALEXANDER PUSHKIN · MAXIM BILLER · JULIEN GRACQ
BROTHERS GRIMM · HUGO VON HOFMANNSTHAL
GEORGE SAND · PHILIPPE BEAUSSANT · IVÁN REPILA
E.T.A. HOFFMANN · ALEXANDER LERNET-HOLENIA
YASUSHI INOUE · HENRY JAMES · FRIEDRICH TORBERG
ARTHUR SCHNITZLER · ANTOINE DE SAINT-EXUPÉRY
MACHI TAWARA · GAITO GAZDANOV · HERMANN HESSE
LOUIS COUPERUS · JAN JACOB SLAUERHOFF
PAUL MORAND · MARK TWAIN · PAUL FOURNEL
ANTAL SZERB · JONA OBERSKI · MEDARDO FRAILE
HÉCTOR ABAD · PETER HANDKE · ERNST WEISS
PENELOPE DELTA · RAYMOND RADIGUET · PETR KRÁL
ITALO SVEVO · RÉGIS DEBRAY · BRUNO SCHULZ · TEFFI
EGON HOSTOVSKÝ · JOHANNES URZIDIL · JÓZEF WITTLIN